ASCENSION SAGA, BOOK 1

INTERSTELLAR BRIDES® PROGRAM: ASCENSION SAGA

GRACE GOODWIN

Published by KSA Publishers
Goodwin, Grace
Interstellar Brides® Program: Ascension Saga Book 1

Publisher's Note:
This book was written for an adult audience. The book may contain explicit sexual content. Sexual activities included in this book are strictly fantasies intended for adults and any activities or risks taken by fictional characters within the story are neither endorsed nor encouraged by the author or publisher.

GET A FREE BOOK!

JOIN MY MAILING LIST TO BE THE FIRST TO KNOW OF NEW RELEASES, FREE BOOKS, SPECIAL PRICES AND OTHER AUTHOR GIVEAWAYS.

http://freescifiromance.com

INTERSTELLAR BRIDES® PROGRAM

YOUR mate is out there. Take the test today and discover your perfect match. Are you ready for a sexy alien mate (or two)?

VOLUNTEER NOW!

interstellarbridesprogram.com

PREQUEL

Twenty-seven years ago Queen Celene was forced to flee Alera with her unborn child. Read the story of her escape to Earth in The Ascension Saga prequel.

QUEEN CELENE, PLANET ALERA, TWENTY-SEVEN YEARS AGO

Darkness surrounded us like a blanket, but the night was not warm. It was cold. Deadly. I stumbled through the alleys and shadows as if I carried a mortal wound.

I did. My heart beat and I was not injured, but I did not feel anything but pain. Loss. And rage. A rage so terrible I knew if I let out the smallest sound I would scream for hours.

"Come, my queen. We are nearly there." The guard's arm around my waist was gentle but firm. I did not know his name. The crest on his uniform was from a family I knew and trusted and for now, that was enough. This young man had saved my life even as my love, my king, lay dead. With each step we took, I moved farther away from my mate, from the life I knew as Queen Celene, the life we shared ruling Alera. Everything had changed now. The planet was in crisis, and I knew what I must do. I would not allow a coup to overthrow the peaceful rule of government which had been established thousands of years before. I would not allow those who wanted me dead to take control.

"There will be warriors not loyal to you guarding the citadel. They won't allow you to just walk inside, to the only safe place for you on the planet. They will either kill you on sight or take you directly to the bastards who slayed the king, who wish you dead as well. Who almost succeeded." The second guard was older, a dear friend for many years, and his harsh words caused me to shudder. Of course, he was correct.

The traitors who wanted me dead would take the sacred gemstones, worn for eons by the planet's current ruler, and try to use them for their own ends. The black stones around my neck were a sign of my reign and were meant to be passed on to my heir, as had been done generation after generation, for longer than our recorded history.

For the first time in my life, I feared that the royal blood I carried would truly face its end. My living cousins had all been tested, and proven not strong enough to carry one of the sacred gifts. I was newly wed to my mate, and the traitors thought to strike now, before an heir could be born. Without a future queen to lead the people, they would be forced to break tradition, to choose a ruler who was weak, not a direct descendant of the ancients.

Tonight, they had nearly succeeded. We faced bleak times on Alera, and it was clear the attempt to overthrow the eons-long rule of my family line, and the sacred gifts we carried, was finally at hand. My enemies had, at last, shown themselves. Killed my king, my love. Tried to kill me.

They wanted the throne.

That I could not allow. Other than the attempted coup this evening, Alera was at peace. It would remain that way as long as I were alive. But in the hands of evil... I shuddered at the thought of what could happen to my home world, of what the wrong heart might do with the technology hidden away in the citadel.

Hearing heavy footfall, I tugged my two guards deeper into the shadows as a group of armed fighters stormed past us in the open street. They were searching for me, no doubt, to take me to those leading the uprising. My lifeforce was all that was separating them from what they wanted.

It was late and most of my people were sleeping soundly in their beds, believing that tomorrow would be just another day. Content. Safe. They were wrong and would hear of my mate's death with the dawn. "We must go in the far entrance," I murmured, tipping my voice low. "Near the water."

"There is no entrance on that side, my queen." The young man offering me support spoke with the surety of youth, perhaps thinking I was actually hurt, that I might have hit my head in the attack. But he was wrong.

"Yes, there is," I replied. "Trust me."

I knew of the entrance because my mother had told me of it, the knowledge passed down from queen to queen, mother to daughter, since the citadel had been built. Ages, eons ago. No one knew the exact date the ancients had erected the mighty tower, nor where the sacred energy that gave the royal heirs their power originated. But one thing was widely known—the citadel protected itself and allowed only those of royal blood to enter the building.

Many others had attempted to cross the threshold. All had met instant death.

I'd not used the hidden entrance since the day

my mother had shown it to me; there had been no need for it. Until now.

"We will get you there, my queen." My old friend looked down at me, his face grave, half covered in shadow. I was grateful for the darkness so that I did not have to look at him. I couldn't look at him. He was covered in blood. The king's blood and his own mixed into a dark cocktail that stained his back and side. He would need a ReGen wand to survive the night.

If the citadel was well guarded—and not by those loyal to me—as he suspected, perhaps none of us would.

But I must survive. There was more than my life at stake.

I nodded at him and stood taller, shrugging off the assistance of the young guard. The shock of seeing my mate murdered before me faded, replaced by determination. I would not fail. Not in this. I must live so Alera would not be overthrown.

I lowered my hand to my abdomen, to the new life stirring there, and covered our daughter, the future queen, with the warmth of my palm. She was new, but her heartbeat was strong. She would have a strong spirit. A will of iron. She would not be broken, and so I would not be broken either.

I would keep her safe at all costs.

"Let's go. Get me to the river. I'll take care of the rest."

"Yes, my queen. This way."

I followed silently as my old friend moved like a phantom from shadow to shadow. The young guard behind me was all but forgotten as the glistening silver spires of the citadel came into view. The ancient structure was built by a race of immortals who had long since disappeared into nothing more than myth, their secrets carried safely by the royal family generation after generation. Hidden. Protected.

The line of succession had been thinned in recent years. An accident had killed my first cousin a year before. His daughter had died a few months later. Suicide. But now, after the attempt on my life and the successful demise of my mate, I had to wonder if she'd killed herself at all. As heavy as the thought made my aching heart, I now knew, beyond a doubt, that someone was trying to end the royal line entirely.

Tonight, they'd almost succeeded, but no one knew of the child I carried. Of the successor to the throne. A direct line would pass to my daughter. I could feel her spirit within, alive with a spark so fierce and bright I would do anything to protect it, including fleeing the only planet I'd ever known. My home. A proud people that I was honored to rule. She was the light that would save this world and these fools from their own stupidity.

When the time was right, we'd return together. I'd lead and groom her to succeed me. Her daughter after her. I had faith in her, in the love that had conceived her.

And if anything happened to me? She would live and she would return to Alera to rule. She would not just return and rule, but seek vengeance for what happened today. For all who had died, her father included. I'd make sure of it.

The silver walls of the citadel sparkled from within whether it was day or night, as if the building were alive. In the front, near the main stairs and entrance, a large garden stretched out for several blocks like a fan of green grass, trees and silken blooms. This late, the moon shone down on the one closest to the entrance, the shimmering, translucent petals of the Aleran flowers so beautiful, so peaceful even as the night exploded in violence throughout the rest of the city.

My mate was dead. Other close family. The royal guard. All gone. And yet the citadel stood, a bastion of strength and promise. All I had to do was hide the royal necklace that held so much power and get my baby somewhere far, far away. Somewhere she could grow strong. Powerful.

I had to flee to a planet so small and insignificant that no one would ever think to look there for us. They would search...and know I was alive. Know the queen still reigned, even in hiding, because of the citadel's beacon of light. The constant glow of the spire would tell Alera their queen still lived.

I tripped on the hem of my jeweled gown and my dear friend caught me as I fell, gently leaning me against the cold, silver wall. "We are here, my queen, but there is no entrance."

I nodded my head and finally looked him in the eye, strong enough now to give him the honor he deserved. "You have served me well, served your king with honor. You are a fine warrior and I am proud to call you friend."

His dark eyes turned grave and he blinked hard, turning away from me so I would not see his tears. "I have failed you. Failed the king."

"No." Grabbing his hand, I placed his palm over the small swell of my abdomen. "No. He lives on. Our daughter grows strong inside me. The family does not fall this night. As long as the spire light burns, know that we live, and we will return."

"What can I do for you, my queen?" He dropped to his knees, swaying there as fresh blood continued to coat his side. Next to him, the young guard dropped to his knees as well.

"What can *we* do?"

"Tell no one that you were with me, that you saw me. Tell no one of the child I carry." I stood as tall as I was able, held my chin high, even as I heard footsteps approach. "And survive. Survive and support my daughter when she returns to seek vengeance."

They both bowed their heads and I used that moment to slip inside the citadel. The entrance was hidden, a field of energy that looked like any other part of the wall. But for those with royal blood, one step was all it took to cross the barrier and enter the inner sanctum.

Outside, I heard the clash of sword on sword, of men yelling. Of death cries. But I didn't dare turn back. If the enemy had arrived, I only had minutes to hide the royal necklace and escape before one of my traitor cousins would arrive and breach the barrier.

When I was sure the gemstones were secure, hidden well and never to be found without my direction, I looked at the sacred spires one last time. Several tiers of sacred stones adorned the precious metal. By some unexplained miracle—the best physicists on the planet had tried to understand for years how the energy of the stones had chosen me and all the queens before—the citadel itself bound to me, to my life force, and the spire would glow with fire no matter where I was in the galaxy, for as long as I drew breath. As long as my body was alive, the stones and I were linked on a quantum level.

I stepped from the hidden room, looked up. Saw my spire, my proof of life, well lit. All the spires were visible for miles, the light a beacon of royal power and strength for eons. In the beginning, all nine spires would glow, the royal bloodline strong. The line of ascension unbreakable.

Over time, something had happened to us. Fewer births. Wars. And now? Now there was only me. But so long as that ray rising out of the spire stayed lit, no one could claim my throne. The spire did not lie. That light, visible for miles, could not be vanquished unless I ceased to draw breath. No one of my living cousins had been deemed worthy by whatever intelligence was buried in the walls of the ancient structure.

But I did not doubt the life force or fire my

daughter would carry. When she returned, I would bring her here, place her blood in the spire next to mine, and hold her to me with joy as we watched her spire glow for all the people to see.

It was time to disappear and wait. To blend in and hide until it was time for my daughter to return. I would need to leave the planet in disguise and not as queen. And so I stripped off my jeweled robes, left them in a pile at my feet. Beneath, a simple shift dress and scarf would allow me to escape unnoticed.

Whoever wanted to overthrow the royal line would not succeed tonight. And the light of the spire would keep my enemies in constant torment until I could avenge my family. Until my daughter ascended.

Heart breaking all over again, I clenched my jaw and straightened my shoulders as I took one last look at the spire's light. I would not be here to lead my people, but they would know I had not abandoned them, would wait for my return.

With one final glance toward the hiding place of the royal necklace, I knew the sacred gemstones would be safe until my daughter's return.

Swallowing my tears, I made my way to the secret exit and disappeared.

TRINITY JONES, PRESENT DAY, INTERSTELLAR BRIDES PROCESSING CENTER, EARTH

The car skidded and the left two wheels lifted off the pavement as I took the corner going hella-fast. My NASCAR skills didn't matter since the black SUV behind us didn't even slow down.

"I need to take more driving lessons," I grumbled, gripping the wheel tighter.

I'd gone to college, law school, and taken basic self-defense, but none of that included stunt driving. Looking back, Mother should have insisted on it the day I turned sixteen.

"God, Trin, you're going to kill us before we get there." My middle sister, Faith—older than her twin by a whopping eight minutes—laughed from the back as she scolded me, her white knuckled death grip on the two front seats the only thing keeping her in the car.

"Just pull over and let me shoot the assholes. *Then* we can go to Alera." And that annoyed voice was my baby sister, Destiny, sitting in the passenger seat petting her gun like it was her favorite kitten. I was past the worry of her shooting me accidentally; she was too skilled. She looked like the more easy-going one of my twin sisters, but she'd spent every day of her life since she was four learning how to fight, hunt, stalk and kill things. The purple hair and huge, innocent looking baby-blue eyes were a total fake-out on any man who thought he had *her* figured out.

Not that she'd let very many try. We'd all dated. We weren't innocent, sequestered virgins. But we *were* princesses. Not that anyone knew it. And not that we'd really, *really* believed it until a few hours ago. There were too many Disney princesses out there for us to have believed we were actual royalty from another planet.

Another freaking planet.

"Just shoot out their tires or something. That's what they do in the movies." Faith was grinning like a maniac, loving the adventure. Unlike Destiny, Faith *looked* innocent. Completely and totally innocent. Long golden brown hair. Warm, dark eyes. She looked like the biggest softie on the planet. And when it came to animals, that was true. She dragged home every sick creature within a ten-mile radius of our house, snakes included. But people? Ouch. Not so much. As twins, they should have been more alike, but they were fraternal and their personalities were as unbelievably different as they looked.

"Don't you dare," I threatened, keeping my eyes on the road. "We're almost there. I can see the parking lot."

"I won't miss, Trin. Let me do it." Destiny was already eyeing the SUV, the road, the angles.

"No. You won't miss." I glanced out the rear-view mirror at the SUV. "They're going too fast. The stupid thing will probably flip and roll and some poor bastard just trying to do his job won't go home to his family tonight. No. This isn't their fight."

With a deep sigh I'd heard hundreds of times, Destiny leaned back in the seat and let me drive. "Fine. Freaking diplomat. For the record, they're chasing *us.*"

Faith turned around and waved at the sunglass-wearing Men-In-Black in the SUV behind us. I had to grin when I saw driver's jaw tighten. "Stop tormenting the alien chasers."

"Spoil-sport."

"Hippie," I fired back.

"And the freak to the rescue!" Destiny let out a yell of victory as I burned rubber making the turn into the parking lot of the Interstellar Brides Processing Center. We weren't brides, exactly. We weren't here to be tested and matched to an alien mate. We *were* the aliens. Sort-of. I was one-hundred-percent alien, according to our mother. But my pain-in-the-ass sisters were only half.

So, we weren't brides. But we weren't going to enter on the military side either. I knew the place processed both warriors and brides for the Coalition Fleet, but I didn't want to explain things to a soldier. While there *were* women soldiers, plenty of them, I didn't have time to deal with a man if one was on duty. And, from what my mother warned when we were younger, my *Aleran Ardor* had begun—a *really* long story—and getting in front of a man wouldn't be the best thing for me right now.

Long story short, if I saw a man I wanted, I'd be aggressive, want to climb him like a monkey, and be totally disappointed and even more needy and in danger when the deed was done. My sisters? Well, we didn't know yet. But *my* body was driving me crazy, and not one man I'd seen had flipped my switch.

Mother insisted I would need the sacred energy of an Aleran male to calm my need, but I hadn't *really* believed *that* either. At least not until I'd tried to quench my thirst with one of the hotties I'd lusted after at work. Big mistake.

I kissed him, and I swear to God his mouth tasted like an ashtray. And he didn't even smoke.

Plus, he'd fallen asleep for four hours after just a couple of kisses. I'd stayed and watched over him, made sure he was still breathing. And given up on ever having sex again on planet Earth. Now that I had to feed this *ardor* thing, I needed an alien man, one I wouldn't drain dry and kill with a bit of kissing.

Damn inconvenient. So, I needed to get to Alera, or die. And we needed to save our mother. We needed transport off this planet. Like *now*.

But first, we had to get past the massive—and massive as in bigger than my mom's Volkswagon massive—alien guarding the gate. I braked to a screeching halt with him in front of my mom's little Beetle. His arms were crossed and he had one mean scowl on his face. He screamed alpha male mixed with giant. That meant he had a giant— Yeah, I didn't need to think about alien men right now, no matter how big or how hot he looked. Stupid alien hormones.

"Holy shit." Destiny's jaw dropped. "Is that an Atlan? I'd heard they were big, but—"

"Hubba-hubba. Trinity, maybe he could help with that itch you want to scratch." From the back seat, Faith waved, a huge, very genuine smile on her face.

"No way," I countered. "Not happening. We've got to get inside and get someone to transport us to Alera. Now. I don't have time to *scratch my itch.*" I was not happy about any of this bullshit, and I didn't want to take a chance. He was magnificent, but he wasn't Aleran. I was afraid I'd kill him, too, no matter how big and fierce he looked.

"Yeah, don't want to give our special friends a show anyway," Faith added. "Let's go!"

As we'd planned—about five minutes ago when the SUV decided to try to stop us from getting here—we figured our best bet was to beg for asylum. Jumping the first huge alien hottie I came across wasn't part of that. "Doesn't look like he's going to let us drive through him."

"Don't you dare hurt a single hair on that magnificent alien's head," Faith ordered. She sighed...*dramatically.* "Damn. I think I need an Atlan."

"Oh hell, no. You're not going into heat, too, are you?" Destiny was serious. And I was worried. They were only three years younger than I was, but Mother had been watching me like a hawk since I'd turned twenty-two, figured I was a *late bloomer* because there were no Aleran males around to rev my engine.

But the twins were half human, so who knew? "Faith?" I asked.

She rolled her eyes. "No, my Vah-Jay-Jay is not melting. I'm fine."

Destiny raised her brows.

"Seriously. I wouldn't lie about it. Not now." She looked over her shoulder at our special friends and grinned. "Looks like they're not sure what the big, bad alien is going to do either."

"They won't wait around forever. Get out," I told them. "Let's run for it."

As if they could hear me, the men behind us opened their car doors and got out, using the doors as shields. The giant in front of us took two steps forward, a frown on his face when he spotted the men climbing from their car. I watched as the duo chasing us looked at each other, trying to decide what to do, whether or not they wanted us badly enough to take on a huge-ass alien.

"Who are they anyway, and why are they after us?" I asked.

"I can go all female Rambo on them," Destiny said, determined. "Just say the word."

I shook my head. "No. The smartest thing is to get the hell off of Earth."

I looked out the windshield and spotted two more big warriors heading in our direction from behind the Atlan. Reinforcements. Apparently, we were drawing a crowd.

"Go!" I didn't have time to worry about whether or not my sisters would listen to me. Our mother was missing. No, not missing. She'd been *taken.* And we were going to get her back.

Grabbing my backpack, I opened the driver's door and ran for the giant as fast as I could. Destiny beat me to him, of course, dashing past him screaming "Sanctuary!" at the top of her lungs. I ran, slightly out of breath by the time I reached him, more from adrenaline than from the distance. But Faith…

"Damn it, Faith! Come *on,* or I'll shoot you myself." Destiny stood between two hulking giants as I stood behind the original alien who'd stopped our car. Faith, however, was barely jogging, swinging her bag in the air, taunting the government, or military, or whoever they hell they were—agents behind her. They could have caught her. Easily. And she *knew* it. But she always loved a good cat and mouse game, and she knew the humans wouldn't want to mess with her with the alien hotness surrounding us.

"I'm coming, I'm coming." She was smiling. Radiant. The giant closest to me stirred to attention, looking at her. With a grin, she patted him on the biceps as she walked past, the top of her head not even coming up to his shoulder. "Thanks, big guy."

"My pleasure, my lady." He bowed slightly to her.

The agents walked forward but stopped at the open doors of our car, peering inside. Perhaps hoping we'd left a decoded message about the alien ship that landed at our house this morning. Insane, right? But no such luck for them. All they'd find were sweaty gym clothes and some mint gum my mom kept in the cup holder.

Still, they lingered. Safe now, sure the aliens wouldn't allow these men to take us anywhere we might not come back from, I stood and watched with my arms crossed.

"Please, Miss Jones. We just want to ask you and

your sisters a few questions." The older agent actually took off his sunglasses. He looked like he was about fifty, his gaze hard, but not evil. He looked like what he was, a warrior. Maybe a different kind than the giants guarding the Coalition building, but a fighter all the same. An Earth warrior of some kind. CIA, NSA, some other letters...

"I'm sorry," I replied. "I told you on the phone, we can't give you any answers."

He took a small recorder out of his pocket and placed it on the hood of the car. No doubt he was taking video as well as audio records. "And your father? What about him? Where is he?"

"Stay away from my dad, you asshole." Destiny took two steps forward, but the warrior standing next to her placed a massive hand on her shoulder to hold her back. She glared up at him, completely unafraid, and shook off his touch. But she stayed. Thank God. I didn't want her to have to face murder charges if she decided she wanted to come back home. *After.*

"Our father is safe. And the problem will be taken care of. You have my word on that, officer..." I doubted he'd give me a name. But he did. Kind of.

"Agent Smith."

"Smith, huh? Right."

"Just as your name is Trinity *Jones*."

"It's on my birth certificate."

"Of course. But we already know your father is not Adam Jones. His name is..." He looked down at an old-fashioned notepad. "His given name is Baxter Adam Buchanan, born in Boston. And your mother..." He looked at his notepad again. "Hmmm. Strange. We can't find any verifiable record of your mother at all. Care to explain that, Miss *Jones*? Or the alien vessel that we tracked to your home early this morning?"

They knew Dad's real name? Shit. They'd dug deeper than I thought in such a short time. Not that it mattered. Nothing mattered now but getting off the planet and finding my mother. Yes, it sounded ludicrous... having to *leave* Earth, but reality proved we weren't Disney princesses.

"No, I don't." I stepped up to the big alien next to me and looked up, way up, into his face. If he'd been angry, or mean, he'd have been ten times scarier than the M-I-B who had just chased us down. But he was neither. He looked, curious—and ready to kill to defend me, which made me feel safer than I had for hours. Since those monsters had stormed the house and grabbed our mother, screaming, from her bed. Had it only been this morning?

"I need to see Warden Egara, please," I told him. "It's an emergency."

While I found him attractive, my desire wasn't all that strong. Sure, I wanted to have a man—or big, hot alien induced orgasm—but it wasn't going to be from him. I saw no interest in his eyes. No heat, only duty. And while the need to fuck grew stronger every day because of the Aleran heat women went into, I wasn't going to get it on with just any big cock. No, it had to be *Aleran* cock. Someone big and powerful and strong enough to survive me.

Inwardly, I rolled my eyes. I didn't have time to be going insane with lust.

The alien bowed at the waist, breaking me from my thoughts. "Of course, my lady." He held out his arm to direct me toward the building, all but ignoring Agent Smith and his sidekick, the other two guards staying behind until my sisters joined me. But Smith wasn't done.

"I'll get answers, Miss Jones," he called. "If not from you, from your father."

At the threat, I turned and let him see the rage in my eyes. "You will have your answers. I will return, Agent Smith. And when I do, if you have hurt one hair on my father's head, I'll kill you myself."

"Not if I find him first." Destiny pulled her gun

from one of the mystery pockets on her leather pants, only to have the giant next to her pluck it from her hands as if taking candy from a baby. She just grinned up at him, not a hint of apology in her eyes. "Sorry about that."

"Earth females," he said, tucking the gun away, far away, from my bloodthirsty sister. Destiny wasn't normally like this. In fact, she was a big softie. But hearing our mother's screams this morning had flipped a switch in all of us.

For years, Mother had told us stories of her home world, of the ancients who had helped her people, bestowed a royal necklace of magical stones upon her ancestors to help our bloodline rule. A citadel only those of royal lineage could enter. Of the attempted coup forcing her to flee, the death of my biological father, the king. How she'd come to Earth and met Adam, fallen in love, married him. Gave birth to Faith and Destiny. But her daughters—all three of us—had never belonged here, on Earth. She'd made that clear since the day we could understand language. In fact, she'd insisted we learn to speak Aleran from her. We weren't completely fluent, and who knew what had gone on there over the last twenty-seven years, but we'd learned everything we could. She'd said our time would come to return to Alera. And now, here we were, whether we liked it or not.

We were royal. We were from an ancient Aleran bloodline. Princesses. Mom hadn't been taken by some idiot home invaders on Earth. The space ship in our front yard proved that. She'd been taken by someone from Alera, from *home.*

Why now? She'd been pregnant with me when she left...twenty-seven years ago. That was a long time for a queen to be in exile.

While we'd lived on Earth our entire lives, it was time for us to return. The people of Alera weren't going to know what hit them when the Jones sisters arrived to find their mother, to *save their queen*.

It was time to go to our home world and kick some serious ass.

1

Trinity Jones, Interstellar Brides Processing Center, Miami

"It's just like getting your ears pierced, my ass," my sister, Destiny, grumbled, her hand covering her neck where the NPU had just been inserted by the biggest needle I'd ever seen go into a conscious person. "That *hurt.*"

She paced the room, as if the pain would go away by walking it off. Her shoulder-length purple hair swayed as she moved.

"Stop whining. I went first." I wasn't about to let my sisters see exactly how nervous I was. As the oldest, I had to keep my shit together. No matter how terrifying the last twenty-four hours had been, I had a feeling the next twenty-four were going to be far worse. "With all those tattoos up and down your spine"—the markings were elaborate, feminine, and very beautiful, but I'd never admit that to her—"you should be used to the tiny little poke of a needle."

Destiny rolled her eyes, still rubbing the area behind her ear. "That wasn't a normal needle. That's a knitting needle shooting tiny bullets into our brains."

Warden Egara, the official representative of the Coalition Fleet at the bride processing center, was from Earth herself, but didn't appear to have much of a sense of humor today. "The NPU doesn't go into your brain, ladies. The nanotech burrows into the temporal bone surrounding the cochlea and transmits modified sounds directly to the cochlear nerve. And you'll all be very thankful when you can understand anyone you come across." She was efficiency personified. Crisp uniform, sleek dark hair, easy-going, yet serious demeanor. And all that science talk? Not my thing, but Faith was nodding with a fascinated look on her face.

Science geek. Faith had been bringing hurt animals and even insects home since she could walk. For all that, she had a gentle spirit that neither

Destiny nor I could claim. I liked order. The rule of law. Tradition. Faith never made plans. And Destiny? Well, my baby sister pretty much walked around beating up bullies and making sure shit got done. Together, we were strong. I just hoped we were strong enough to survive the next few weeks. Hell, years. We were going home to a planet none of us had ever seen. And we were hunting for enemies we didn't know.

The whole thing was a giant cluster-fuck, and I wished I'd listened to Mother two years ago when she suggested we return to Alera. But I'd been in law school. Too busy. Always too busy.

Now she was gone, and it was my fault.

"Stop being a baby or you'll scare Faith," I said. The injection *had* hurt, but since I'd gone first, I'd bit my lip and stifled my gasp at the sharp pain. Really, there should be a numbing solution, or some kind of drug for this.

"Just because I like to dress like a girl doesn't mean I'm not tougher than both of you." My middle sister, Faith, was eight minutes older than her twin. Both of them were almost three years younger than my twenty-seven. They were my half-sisters, but their human father wasn't the reason we were all here—getting ready to transport to another world sight unseen.

Faith took a deep breath, let it out, as Warden Egara prepared the wicked looking tool for her turn. It *was* like an ear-piercing gun, but with a needle meant for an amniocentesis or alien probing instead of adding studs to a little girl's earlobes at the local mall's jewelry kiosk.

"Don't faint. I'm in too much pain to catch you," Destiny taunted.

"Spare me the drama," Faith said to Destiny, who still held her hand over the spot where the NPU had been placed. As Warden Egara stepped closer, Faith swung her long, brown hair up over her opposite shoulder to bare the spot needed for the injection. "Mother taught us the Aleran language, Warden. I'm not sure why this is necessary."

The whistle of pressurized air moving through the needle made me wince right along with Faith as the NPU pierced her skin. "There are over two hundred and sixty worlds out there with thousands of languages. Most worlds are not like Earth; they are much more advanced and welcome travelers from other planets."

In other words, Earth was a primitive, unenlightened and unimportant place in the grand scheme of things. Mother had told us she wanted to hide on a planet so far removed from the politics and bullshit of the Interstellar Coalition that she'd chosen Earth for those very reasons. No one in almost thirty years had thought to look for her here. Until I'd screwed up and called Warden Egara a few days ago. Asked for some information on Alera and the ridiculous Aleran Ardor mother had insisted I was coming down with.

My body was going haywire and I got desperate. Stupid lack of discipline and a mistake I wouldn't make again. One stupid phone call, and they'd come for our mother within two days.

Mother. Shit. She was out there somewhere. The small space ship that had been in our front yard gave me hope that she was still alive. They'd broken into our home in broad daylight while my sisters and I were at work. Dad had been asleep on the couch. And later, watching the surveillance video from our home security system, my sisters and I learned they'd pointed some kind of stun gun at him to keep him asleep. The aliens had landed, put the drop on Dad, shot Mother with some sort of light blast, and carried her unconscious body out to their ship.

She'd been limp when they took her. No blood

that we could see on the video, but that didn't mean she was still alive.

In fact, if what Mother told us about the light of the sacred spires on Alera was true, I had a feeling whoever took her might *want* her dead.

Alera. The planet was one our mother had spoken of for as long as we could remember. But we all grew up just like normal kids. Dad had officially adopted me when I was two. Mother had married him and then had my twin sisters. We all went to school. Typical stuff like science fair projects, prom. Graduated. I went on to law school, like our dad. Faith was a biologist with a strange title working for the forest service. And Destiny? Well, Destiny was our battle specialist. We'd all been trained in basic martial arts from a young age, but for Destiny, fighting was like breathing. She loved it. And she was damn good at it. She managed a dojo and taught classes six days a week. She was so toned that watching her move was like watching a wild tiger, light on her feet but scary as hell.

Unless our house had been part of a sci-fi movie set we didn't know about, the Alerans had finally come for our mother. Bad guy Alerans. After years of listening to Mother talk about her home planet—*our* planet—I knew we were the good guys.

And now they had her. Why? I had no clue, but I wasn't going to sit on Earth and twiddle my thumbs. We were her daughters. We *had* to find her.

I knew what she'd say. I was heir apparent. It was my *duty* to go to Alera and take my rightful place. Period. No searching for her. No trying to save her. She'd scold us all and insist that the future of Alera was most important.

Yeah, no. Not to me. And not to my sisters.

Dad was staying here, on Earth, until we contacted him with news. The Alerans didn't know my sisters and I existed. I'd never understood Mother's insistence that we have no family photos on the walls, no school pictures. Our rooms had always looked like guest rooms. Pretty, but not personal. We didn't leave our clothes out. Or our shoes. There weren't toothbrushes or makeup on the counters in the bathroom.

Our house looked like a guest house. A vacation rental. Always.

I'd hated it growing up. Capital H. But now I understood. They'd taken her and hadn't even looked for anyone else. Had no idea she had children. Daughters.

Heirs.

But if she had been taken by Alerans, and we all

agreed she had—me and my sisters, plus Warden Egara and even Prime Nial, the ruler of Prillon Prime and The Colony—we had to find her *on* Alera. Why would they stay on Earth? They knew nothing of the planet. Staying on Earth did them no good. Even if they killed her, they'd go back to Alera and reap their reward.

"Does this work on animals? Think of how amazing that would be. The symbiosis of the universe would be... complete," Faith said, angling her head to the side to give the warden better access so she could wipe the spot with some rubbing alcohol.

Destiny was still pacing, a bundle of raw nerves. "Symbiosis? Really? They could be torturing our mother right now and you're thinking about communing with animals? Do you imagine the bad guys even consider symbiosis? Hell, would they even know what it means?"

"No." Faith grinned, completely unrepentant. "But Trinity certainly does." Faith glanced at me, her hand going to the side of her head. She'd switched into speaking Aleran. "With her super-sexy *Ardor* coming on, she'll want some serious *symbiosis* with a hot alien hunk as soon as we get to Alera."

I rolled my eyes as Destiny waggled her brows

and grinned. "Oh, yeah. Hot, sweaty, symbiosis. Probably more than once."

"I can understand you," Warden Egara added. "And I've shared the details of Trinity's oncoming Aleran Ardor with Prime Nial—"

I groaned, blushing. I didn't need everyone in the universe to know my pussy was wet all the time and aching for a huge cock. That I was becoming a horny slut, eager for a male to take me for a wild ride. Earth guys wouldn't do. I'd tried that. Ten minutes of making out like high schoolers and my poor date had collapsed, unconscious, on his couch. I was like a freaking sexual vampire. Afraid I'd killed him, I stayed for a bit just watching him breathe. That had scared the hell out of me and I'd called the Interstellar Brides processing center first thing the next morning.

And given away mother's location. Got her kidnapped. Tortured. Shit, maybe dead.

"Don't, Trin. I can see it all over your face. This isn't your fault." Faith shook her head, giving me her very best motherly impression.

"It kinda is, Faith."

"Bullshit, Trin. Biology. That's all this is. Maybe we should just get you taken care of here. There's got to be a few hunky aliens around who wouldn't mind a quickie."

"I don't need a quickie. Thanks though." No. Nothing quick would do. I needed a big Aleran male to shove me up against the wall and do me. Hard. *Really hard.* For *hours.*

God, I clenched my inner walls, aching and eager to be filled. This mating urge was getting out of control, but I clenched my teeth—and other places—and ignored it. *Again.*

"—and Prime Nial has assured me he will have an official Aleran consort waiting for you in the transport center," the warden continued. "I don't know much about Alera, but I've been assured your Ardor will be soothed by the consort." She offered me a small smile.

"You're kidding," Destiny said, looking at me. "Did you know about this? It sounds like a male prostitute."

Warden Egara shook her head. "More like an escort, although there really isn't an equivalent on Earth."

I was sure they could hear my sigh in the next room. "Yes. Mother told me. They are very rare and extremely expensive." Having sex immediately upon arrival with a complete stranger? Not my thing, but my body was telling me otherwise. I was so amped up, I wasn't going to have a choice.

"Hey, wait," Destiny said, holding up her hand, the big needle all but forgotten. "You're speaking Aleran, Warden. How can you do that? How can you understand us? I mean, you're from Earth. You're *on* Earth."

Warden Egara turned and put the NPU gun away. "I was tested as a bride, given an NPU and matched to Prillon Prime. I had two mates who died in the war. When I chose not to mate again, I came back to Earth to help new brides find their mates." She turned around, glanced at each of us, put her fingers to the spot behind her ear. "And you three? I admit, you're definitely a surprise."

"I'm sorry." Always the peacemaker, but I had to say it. How sad. Two mates who died must be devastating for her.

Her smile was resigned. "It was a long time ago. And now, you three need to get moving."

"Yeah, a secret Aleran princess, hiding away on Earth, waiting to ascend the throne," Faith replied, noticing the way the warden had switched topics and clearly didn't want pity or additional conversation about her dead mates. "Trin, your life is like a romance movie."

"Except Mother's been taken and I can't control my own freaking body," I countered. "It's more like an action-adventure-horror." My stomach twisted, remembering the way the blood had drained from my head when we watched the surveillance video, heard her scream of rage right before they'd shot her. Her instant collapse onto the kitchen floor. The way she'd slumped like a wet spaghetti noodle.

She'd hit her head on the corner of the cabinet on her way down. And I didn't know if it was the twisted version of heat I was in or just my natural rage, but someone was going to pay for that. I wasn't normally violent, but I had my moments. And this Aleran Ardor was not only inconvenient, it was flat out pissing me off. *Forced* to fuck or go insane?

What kind of messed up biology did these stupid aliens have, anyway?

"Prime Nial won't be there to meet you himself as he's on Prillon, three sectors away from Alera, but he will have a contingent of guards as well as the Aleran consort waiting to greet you."

"It's hard to think about this Ardor thing when my mother's missing," I said. I rubbed my hands on my jeans, realized I'd thrown clothes on this morning and hadn't even brushed my hair in our mad dash to get to the Brides center. There was no way a consort was going to want to get it on with me looking like this. I tugged at the hem of my t-shirt and realized it was inside out. *Fuck.*

"Your Ardor started a few weeks ago. It was coming on whether Mom was taken or not," Destiny replied. "Just think, if you'd been on Alera, this *heat* thing wouldn't have been delayed until you were twenty-flipping-seven." She waved her hand around in reference to the *heat* thing. It was easy for her to be blasé about it since she hadn't come into her Ardor. She didn't have a complete stranger waiting to fuck her brains out so she could *stop going crazy.* "I mean, if it had come on when you were twenty-two, like mother said it should, then you wouldn't have slept with Aiden Dugen."

Aiden Dugen. I had to laugh. Hindsight was definitely twenty-twenty. My college boyfriend should have been avoided. As for his cock, yeah, he would never be mistaken for a hot alien hunk. Hell, a *hunky* anything.

"Yeah, but that hot Atlan at the gate is probably hung like a horse," Faith added, fanning herself with her hand. "If I'd known the aliens were that hot, I might have volunteered to be an Interstellar Bride."

"If we stay on Alera, you'll end up married to an alien," Destiny said. "I think that qualifies."

"Well, being only half Aleran, we don't know if you two are going to have to deal with this stupid Ardor. I hope you don't. I almost killed my coworker last week just *kissing* him," I reminded them.

"That Atlan at the gate can go beast," the warden added. "While that might sound hot and sexy, I can't allow you to mindlessly seduce an honorable warrior and then head off to Alera. He'll demand much more than you want to give. He's not just a big cock to ride. You'd get mating cuffs and a hulking beast obsessed with you for the rest of your life. Not fair to either one of you if you just need that Ardor eased."

I stared at the warden for a second, totally surprised she'd used the phrase *big cock to ride* in a sentence. And *mindlessly seduce an honorable warrior?* "I would never be that dishonest, with any male. Alien or not."

"Good." The warden's brows were up and her lips were tight. Clearly, she had not appreciated Faith's joke.

"Yeah, talk about bossy. That Atlan looked like a total alpha male. Probably *way* too bossy," Faith added with a sigh that sounded suspiciously like longing. She tucked her dark hair behind her ear, then gave a little wince when she bumped the NPU injection site. "Even with a big cock to ride."

She glanced to Warden Egara, who smiled in return.

"I'm not going to have a quickie with the Atlan guard just because my girl parts are craving what he's got in his pants," I said on a little laugh, squirming as I thought of *exactly* what he had in those uniform pants. The bulge couldn't have been missed by any woman within thirty feet.

"Fine. The Aleran consort then. While you're getting it on with Mr. Studly, we'll do some investigating." Destiny swung her arm over Faith's shoulders and they both nodded.

"Right," Faith added with a grin. "I don't want to listen to your screams of pleasure. I might get jealous."

I had no intention of going off with an Aleran version of a gigolo who was paid to give me a bunch of orgasms—all while my sisters searched for our mother. That was ridiculous. I'd been horny and eager for sex for weeks. I'd just... ignore it. Like I had been. Or I could just make myself come. It wasn't like I didn't have a vibrator in my bedside table. There had to be a place to pick one up on Alera, along with a whole bunch of batteries.

Taking matters into my own hands had helped... for a while. Lately, it would take the edge off, but seemed to only make my need, my craving, grow worse.

"Warden." A woman in a matching gray and burgundy uniform to Warden Egara's came into the room. "Coordinates are set for Alera; the transport room is ready."

I glanced at my sisters. This was it. We were leaving Earth and going into outer space. To *another planet.*

Oh my god. It was one thing to have my mother talk about Alera. To speak Aleran. We'd used it as our secret language at school and no one knew a thing we were saying. Everything our mother had told us had all seemed like just stories. A game. Fun.

But now it was real. Really, *really* real.

"Holy shit," Destiny said.

"Yeah, holy shit," Faith added as we followed Warden Egara down a long hallway.

The transport room was similar to a *Star Trek* episode. A woman in uniform stood behind a table covered in various controls. Before her was a raised dais with steps leading up to it. Nothing else was in the room.

There was a hum in the air, a vibration beneath

our feet. I looked down at my old sneakers, Faith's sandals and Destiny's black shit-kicking boots. I wondered if I should bother fixing my inside-out shirt.

Shit. Why bother? According to Warden Egara, the second we got there some alien *consort* was just going to strip me out of my clothes anyway. Ugh. Just... shit. I knew I couldn't say no and stay sane. Hell, I was pretty damn sure I wouldn't want to.

Destiny took my hand. Faith, the other. We looked to each other, then climbed the steps, turned around.

We were on the transport pad, the portal to another planet. To *Alera.*

"Good luck on your search for your mother," Warden Egara said. She stood tall, hands folded in front of her, and didn't speak about our heritage, or the fact that our mother was the queen. There were only two people who knew the truth—the warden and Prime Nial. And that's the way we intended to keep it. At least for now. "Please, be safe and let me know how things go. I will be rooting for you."

"Thank you," I replied, my sisters nodding.

She looked to the transport tech person and nodded. The hum got louder, the vibrations intensifying. The hair on the back of my neck stood on end. I felt the tight squeeze of my sisters' hands in mine. We were doing this. Together. Now. We would find our mother… alive, and beat the crap out of those who'd taken her. Make things right. Put Queen Celene back where she belonged, on the throne of Alera.

The Jones sisters were headed to Alera. Those alien kidnappers had no idea what they were in for.

"Your transport will begin in three, two, one…"

The warden's voice faded. Piercing cold felt like a thousand frozen needles pressing into my flesh. My last thought was that the NPU injection hadn't been that bad after all.

2

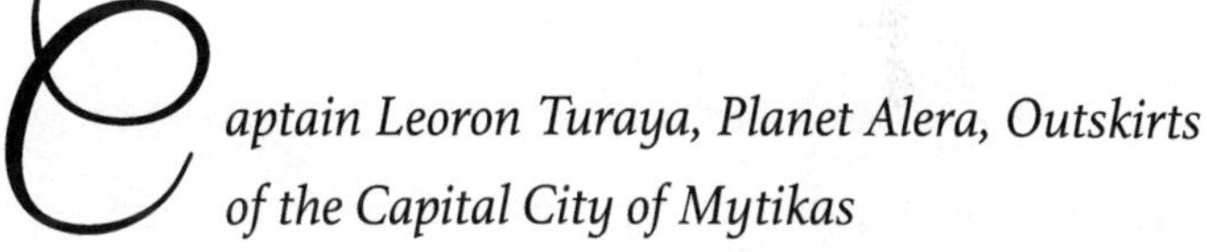

Captain Leoron Turaya, Planet Alera, Outskirts of the Capital City of Mytikas

THE SKY WAS black but for the stars as I stood watch on the outermost tower protecting the capital. No moonlight tonight, the darkness feeling like an omen.

"It's late, Captain. The watch is mine now." Gadiel was young, barely out of training, but he stood at attention ready to assume my position on watch. His gaze was full of honor and excitement, a look I well-remembered seeing in the mirror. That was before I joined the Coalition Fleet and spent nearly a decade fighting a horror worse than any I could have imagined. I'd seen the Hive, knew what they would do if they ever reached the peaceful planets within the protective arms of the Interstellar Coalition's Fleet of battleships.

After ten years, my father had called me home. I could continue to serve on Alera, he argued. I would have fought for ten more, but my parents still hoped I would awaken to a woman's Ardor, that I would choose a mate—or my cock would—and give them grandchildren to spoil.

I'd met countless women in my lifetime, all across the galaxy, and nothing had stirred within me. My body remained mine alone. And to be perfectly honest, I did not hold much interest in changing that. To be so obsessed with a single female? I'd seen mighty Aleran warriors fall, become nothing more than besotted fools. All because their cocks rose—finally—for The One. To be led around by the balls by a female was not what I desired. To be driven by something other than the honor to defend my planet? No, thank you.

I would remain a soldier, a guard, a fighter for life. An Aleran bachelor. Unaffected by the whims of a female.

"Sir?" Gadiel shifted uncomfortably, and I realized I had been staring into the distance, at nothing. No. Not nothing. The spire. That damn queen's spire and how it glowed bright, the only thing illuminating the darkness.

"Very well," I replied, turning to him. "May the light keep you."

"And you as well."

I nodded in acceptance of his words and left him to attend his duties. The city was at peace, at the moment. The last incursion by an outlying family had ended in bloodshed just weeks before. The tenuous peace would not last. The royal bloodline was weak, with no living members strong enough to carry one of the gifts. Ever since the queen's disappearance over two decades ago, the capital had been under consistent attack by one grasping family after another. These families believed their wealth and armies would grant them the loyalty of the people.

They were wrong. So long as the queen's spire burned bright, the royal guard would defend her throne so that one day she might return to reclaim her place among her people. I had lost hope, for I barely remembered a time before she disappeared, but I would fight until the light of the spire died. When that happened, I would fight for the people in my city, choose a family to rule I found worthy. The battles would be bloody, but currently three families held the wealth and power to potentially ascend to the throne. The day the light of the spire went out would be the first day of a very long, very brutal war.

The tower stairs were dark, but I had no trouble seeing my way as I paced through the shadows. There was no need to count the twisting steps, for I'd been this way hundreds of times since my return from space, from the Hive wars.

It seemed my entire life would be dedicated to battle and blood.

So be it. Gods, I was a broody fucker. I needed an Aleran ale, an hour with the hottest setting on my shower tube and my bed. In that order.

Exiting the base of the watchtower, I slowed my pace, in no hurry to return to my quarters. Below me, surrounded by the twisting alleyways and dense tapestry of stone homes, the royal citadel glowed in the center of the city. The strange tower had been there longer than our people had kept records, built by an ancient race of space explorers who left our primitive planet with two gifts—the citadel itself and those who carried their alien bloodline.

The citadel was both a beacon of hope to all of Alera and a bitter reminder that our people had been abandoned when I was a child. I barely remembered the day the king was found dead, the queen missing. My father, now a retired captain of the city guard, still clung to his faith that the royal bloodline lived on, that his beloved queen would return to free us from the chaos of endless civil conflict.

The light shined, so Queen Celene was alive.

But where?

And why had she yet to return?

The younger generation had given up hope. War was coming, no matter how valiantly the clerics fought to keep the peace. I wanted no part in it. The rich fools would fight over something they could never hold. There would be no ascension ceremony, no new queen, not while the light of the spire shined over Mytikas. Queen Celene's city.

As if the thought had garnered the attention of Fate herself, the NPU implanted behind my ear buzzed with an incoming message.

"Prime Nial of Prillon Prime." The voice ringing in my ear was clipped and professional, not asking permission to send the communication through so much as warning me that the comm was coming.

I stilled. "Prime Nial?"

The night was not cold, but a shiver of dread raced over my skin as I waited for the most powerful male in the galaxy to talk to me. Gods, why was he calling me? Now?

Prime Nial ruled not just Prillon Prime, but the entire Interstellar Coalition and its fleet of warships. The Coalition military, made up of at least two hundred fifty planets, was his to command in our war with the Hive.

Epic responsibility and power, and he was wishing to speak with me.

I owed him a life debt. My blood turned to ice in my veins. What was so wrong that he would need to call in that mark? What did he need, a man with so much power? How could he need the assistance of a lowly soldier? I was nothing more than a pawn on Alera. In the grand scheme, I was as small as an insect.

"Prime Nial? This is Captain Leoron Turaya. How may I assist you?" My voice cut through the night.

"Leo? Can you hear me?" The Prime's voice was deeper than I remembered, and the faint sound of a female in the background drifted to me across the vast expanse of space.

"Tell him to hurry. I don't trust those people," she said. Didn't trust who? What was going on?

"Yes, sir. What can I do for you?" How the hell

was he placing a direct call to my NPU? The neural processing unit was standard issue for everyone in the Coalition Fleet, and most diplomats from the individual planets chose to have them inserted as well. Universal translators, they made communication across all the races easy, but I'd had no idea the Fleet could transmit directly to me from halfway across the galaxy. From the ground to a ship? Yes. But from Prillon Prime into my skull?

"I have a very important, extremely delicate task for you, Leo. Are you alone?"

I spun in a slow circle, checking my surroundings. I was on the side of a mountain in the middle of the night at the base of a watchtower. Every sane person on this side of the planet was asleep right now. Besides Gadiel far above me, but he was too distant to overhear. "Yes, Prime Nial. I am completely alone. How may I be of service?"

He cleared his throat and I clenched my teeth. I knew Nial well from my fighting days. He'd saved my life, and I'd sworn to answer his call if he needed me. "Don't call me Prime, Leo."

I couldn't help the way the corner of my mouth tipped up. He might be Prime, but he always said he was just a Prillon warrior saving the Coalition from the Hive, just like any other.

"Fine, *Nial*," I replied, ensuring deference could still be heard. "I have not forgotten the life debt I owe. Ask for anything. It will be yours."

His sigh made my head hurt. "I am transporting three women to Mytikas within the hour. I'm sending you the location of the specific transport station now."

The coordinates were recited in my ear by the transport computer and I recognized the location. "That's on the opposite side of the city."

"Can you arrive in time?"

I looked out over the quiet city streets. Mytikas was a sprawling metropolis that filled the valley between two mountain ranges. "Yes. It will be close, but I can be there in an hour." I'd need to run down the mountain and break a few laws when I reached my EMV, but the vehicle was fast. I'd make it.

"Thank the gods." I could hear the relief in his voice.

"He can get there? They're going to need help. And I don't like the idea of them transporting to a strange planet without someone there we trust." The woman's voice was louder now, and soft, but not tender. Hers was a voice accustomed to giving orders.

"Yes, love," Nial said. "Leo will be able to meet

them." *That* tone was one I'd never heard from him before, and I almost didn't recognize his voice. He sounded... gentle. Which, when I thought of the giant Prillon warrior, was not a word I had ever associated with him before.

"Thank god," the female continued. "Especially with Trinity's little *problem.*"

"Congratulations on your mating, Nial," I said. He'd called her *love,* which let me know exactly who the new Prime was talking to. Lady Jessica Deston, his mate. I assumed his second was nearby. And what problem?

"Thank you," he replied. "How did you hear the news? Alera is far from Prillon Prime."

I laughed, the sound bursting out of me. "Everyone in the galaxy heard about it, you lucky bastard. If you didn't want everyone to know, you and Ander shouldn't have claimed the beautiful lady in the fighting arena during a live, interplanetary broadcast." I'd watched the entire event of the two Prillon males claiming their female. Sacred and erotic, there was no doubt Jessica belonged to Nial and Ander. I was happy for my friend, but had felt nothing as I watched the ceremony. The female he'd been matched to via the Interstellar Brides Program, a woman from Earth, was striking, and very responsive to her mates as they'd claimed her. I'd been pleased that Nial had found happiness, but my body remained as it had always been, dormant.

While a Prillon was connected to his mate and his second by collars that shared feelings, emotions and even sensations, an Aleran male had no such connection. Finding a mate was not easy, especially when an awakening only occurred for The One. And *only* for her. My cock would not rise until she was before me. Oh, I could feel a shadow of desire, stroke my length in anticipation of sinking into my mate's tight pussy, but there would be no completion, no satisfaction, until I was buried deep between her thighs. Only then would I come for the first time.

I knew how to fuck a female—in theory—I just hadn't done it yet. Besides witnessing other claiming ceremonies like Prime Nial's, all males on Alera had attended classes for such things. For while it might take decades for our cocks to awaken to The One, it was crucial we could satisfy our female when the time came. Once a cock was awakened, it would rule a male, drive him to fuck his mate hard and often. Failing to bring a mate her pleasure was a great dishonor, and every male's greatest fear.

Until my body awakened, I was solely a vessel for work, not pleasure.

"Yes," Nial replied. "Well, how could I resist?" His own laughter made me smile, his obvious happiness with his mate coming through loud and clear. Being Prillon, he wouldn't have had a dormant cock like an unmated Aleran male, but I had no doubt the first sight of his matched mate had made his cock rise and, most likely, had yet to go down.

"Not to distract, Nial, but who is Trinity? And what problem?"

"Yes. That." He cleared his throat. "As I said, I am sending three women to Alera. They are to be protected with your life. Do you understand? Every resource you can bring to bear, every friend, every weapon and loyalty you owe me is to be given to these females from Earth. They must be guarded at all costs."

My mind raced. Women from Earth? Coming to Alera? With Prime Nial's personal protection?

"It will be my honor," I told him. "I give you my word. But I don't understand. Who are they? And why are females from Earth coming here?"

Earth was a primitive planet, not yet a full member of the Interstellar Coalition. They were probationary members, and wouldn't have been contacted for another century, at least, if not for the Hive threat so close to them. I had not even heard of an Earth female being matched through the Interstellar Brides Program to a male from Alera.

Nial's mate must have been listening, because she answered my question. "They're from Earth, Leo, which means they're mine. My people. They need to be protected. Okay?"

I answered in her strange Earth slang. "Okay. I give you my word as well. I will protect them with my life."

"Thank god." There she went again, thanking a male deity while all in divinity knew the creator was feminine. Strange creatures, Earthlings. "Now, about Trin's problem, she's got some kind of mating fever, like an Atlan, but not exactly. She almost killed some poor guy back home, sucked him dry, you know?"

What the fuck was this female talking about? How did a small, soft, gentle female *suck* a man to death? Did Jessica mean this Trinity female sucked an Earth male's cock too hard? Were Earth males so weak that they'd die from something I'd heard was extremely pleasurable? Was this Earth female *too good* at the task? I palmed my cock through my pants, wondering what it would feel like to have a hot, wet mouth taking me deep.

"No. I do not," I answered, for I was completely

confused. My cock didn't stir at the thought, but I was curious.

Nial interrupted. "Trinity's got Aleran Ardor. Don't ask me to explain how a female from Earth has this condition, because I'm not able. The human males don't have enough energy to sate her body's growing lust without dying, so I've asked Lord Jax to send a few guards as well as a—what did he call it?"

"A consort," his mate answered. "Someone she can have hot sex with so she can calm down. He better be really good, Nial. This consort better have the moves of a Chippendale dancer and the cock of a stallion because I can't just hand her over like a prize to some freakshow alien who's not worthy."

My brows raised in shock. I had no idea what a Chippendale was, nor whether a stallion had a big cock or not. I had to assume it was large. Mine was, running down my thigh, snug in my uniform pants. And that wasn't even hard. Would an Earth female require more to be satisfied? Their soldiers in the ReCon teams were not overly large. Perhaps their females' anatomy was strange, made to accommodate extremely well-endowed males.

But no. I had seen Earth members of ReCon in the cleansing units—and for the most part—been less than impressed with the sizes of their cocks. Alerans were much, much larger.

The use of a consort was not an uncommon practice. Older males who had lost a mate did not lose their physical ability to lay with females of our species. In young, wealthy families in particular, when a female's Ardor began, and she did not want to interview males for a mate, she would utilize the services of a consort.

They were not cheap, yet I had heard the females were well-satisfied. In fact, the consort's value to the royal families was so high that widowed males often petitioned one of the noble houses for comfort and protection in exchange for their services.

Consorts were rare. Expensive. And not normally on formal standby for alien females to fuck on demand.

Who *were* these three females?

"Leo? You there?"

"Yes."

"Can you get to the transport center? Lord Thordis Jax is sending the consort and five of his personal guards to meet them. Their arrival is to be kept a secret. No one can know who they are or where they came from."

While I knew they came from Earth, I had no

idea *who* they were. It would be an easy task to fulfill. "Understood. Does Lord Jax know you have contacted me?"

Nial laughed again, and if I'd been close enough, I would have punched him in the shoulder as I'd done in years past. "Of course not. I know him, but I don't know his family. I don't know his guards. I don't trust them, not the way I do you. I don't trust anyone fully in this, no one but you. Keep the women safe. Make sure Trinity gets her Ardor under control, and then help the females do whatever they need to do on Alera. Help them. No questions."

"I give you my word."

"Keep them alive."

"Is someone trying to kill them?"

"Yes. And I do not want them to be found. That is all you need to know."

Strange. But I was a soldier, well-used to taking orders. I was not going to argue or ask questions, especially not with the leader of the galaxy asking me for a personal favor. "I'll be at the transport center in an hour."

"Hey, Leo?" Jessica's voice had changed, gone deeper, sultry. "When you run into them, they won't trust you, so we're using Trinity's favorite food as a code word. Strawberry ice-cream. Got it? You say that and she'll know I sent you."

"Yes, my lady."

"Good," Nial said. "One more thing, Leo. If Lord Jax betrays me, kill him."

Fuck. The Jax family was extremely wealthy and powerful, and the Prime of Prillon had just given me permission to murder their prodigal son. Who *were* these humans? And who was going to come looking for them here? On Alera?

Who was irrelevant. They were mine to protect, so I would. "Understood."

"Thank you. One hour." The strange buzzing in my head ceased, leaving me with nothing but the quiet songs of the night insects and the pounding of my own pulse in my ears. Three females from Earth, one who needed to be fucked, and soon. Not my usual guard duty, but I was up for the task. I shifted my cock in my uniform pants. No, *I* wasn't up for it, but the consort would be.

3

Trinity, Planet Alera, Mytikas City, Transport Room

I STAGGERED on the transport pad as the cold faded from my bones, the pinprick pain of dead limbs coming back to life making me want to curl up in a ball and cry. Glancing at Faith and Destiny, I could tell they were having the same miserable sensations.

"Okay?" I asked.

They nodded, wiggled their arms, rolled their heads in circles to loosen their neck muscles.

The transport room looked just like the one on Earth, but like Dorothy in *The Wizard of Oz,* we weren't in Kansas anymore. Yet the Aleran males in front of us were definitely not Munchkins. They were big. Not Atlan big like the guard on Earth, but they gave lumberjacks a run for their money.

Grim gazes of six Aleran males stared at us.

"Welcome to Alera," one of them said.

God, Alera. We really were here. I looked behind me. A wall. Yeah, not Earth. There was no going back now since we were light years away. Not time zones, but a galaxy stood between us and the only life we'd ever known. We were in our own sci-fi movie, and I wasn't Princess Leia. I bit my lip, a little freaked out.

Alera.

It must have been the transport that had muddled my emotions because I was strangely on the verge of tears. What a damn mess. This morning, I was heading off to work and now we were on Alera trying to find our kidnapped mother. And that wasn't all. Everyone in this room expected me to fuck a stranger tonight. Now. An alien. A male I'd never met and might never see again.

Talk about romantic… not. I wasn't a virgin, but I didn't fuck strangers either. I'd never had a one-night stand, never was into casual. No friends with benefits. If my body wasn't such a screaming mess,

I'd send the gigolo—no, consort—on his way and focus on finding my mother.

And this consort? The guy I was supposed to get naked and horizontal with as soon as humanly possible? It was pretty obvious who he was. The other five wore identical uniforms and stood a step behind him. The consort was attractive, muscular, and at least twenty years older than me. He looked like he was about fifty with dark hair and streaks of gray at the temples. He wore a nice suit of some kind. Navy blue. His shoulders were broad and his eyes were kind. That would help. Thank god this whole Ardor thing only happened once. Like losing my virginity with an alien bang. Once the Ardor was over, I could go about my business. Settle down later. I'd be fine. If I survived this without dying of embarrassment.

"Ladies, I am Cassander of the Jax family. It is my pleasure to serve." The consort bowed low at the waist and swept his arms out to include the guards. "These fine warriors are loyal servants of Jax. We are at your service."

His voice was deep. Assured. Calm.

Maybe fucking him would be more like a gyno visit. Efficient. Gentle. Fast.

Over.

If I'd met the consort on the street, I would have thought he looked great for his age. He was huge, just like the guards surrounding him, but markedly older. A silver fox, my mother would have said.

The guards however, were younger. Dressed for duty, their dark uniforms fit to every curve and bulge of muscle and... other things. I looked away quickly and found Destiny watching me.

"Too bad you can't get it on with one of the guards. Holy hotness."

"Shut up." As a comeback, it was pathetic. As in second grade pathetic. But it was all I had at the moment.

"Leave her alone. Let's get Trin's sexy times done so we can do what we came here to do." Faith crossed her arms as she stepped down off the transport and walked up to the guard closest to her. "I assume we aren't expected to stay in this transport station."

"Of course not. We have secured accommodations for the night. We are to remain on guard until Consort Cassander is no longer needed." The guard bowed slightly, but more a bow of respect to a lady than respect to a superior. My shoulders relaxed and a bit of the tension left my spine. Good.

These guys were here, following orders, but they had absolutely no idea who we were. Prime Nial had kept his word.

I doubted we looked like royalty. Hell, my shirt was on inside out. I had to wonder if Cassander even found me appealing. Would he *want* to have sex with me? When was the last time I'd shaved my legs?

But wait. What? "Until he's no longer needed?"

I looked at the consort, who was watching me, his gaze roaming my body. The professional interest I'd read in his eyes before had changed to something more. Something I didn't care for at the moment. Lust. Eagerness. I had become a random piece of ass and it was his job to tap it.

Great. Just great.

"It depends on the female, my lady," Cassander replied. "Some require two days of my attention. Some as many as four. Only you will know when all your needs have been met. I promise I will meet every one of them."

Gag. My need was to get away from this guy and fast.

"Jesus, Trin. Four days? We don't have time for that," Destiny said, always blunt. Unfortunately, she was right. Or fortunately, because if I had to get it on with this guy, I wanted it to be one and done. Like in one hour. Not four fricking *days*.

"What happens if I leave after one day, even if I don't feel—satisfied? What happens?"

He looked shocked, as if he'd never been asked that before. What? Obviously, everyone else wanted to just lounge in bed having sex for days on end. Not me.

Shit. When I thought of it that way, it did sound insane. What woman in their right mind didn't want to do nothing but fuck... again and again? This consort's entire job was to make sure I was satisfied in every possible way. That meant this would be me time. Anything and everything I wanted.

I'd just have to keep my eyes closed and pretend I actually wanted him to be... touching me. As if he could read my mind—and was insulted—he straightened and puffed out his chest. Great. Even consorts had easily wounded male egos. "If you leave before you are fully sated, your relief will only be temporary. You will quickly return to your former state," he said, his voice full of reassurance.

"How quickly?" If I had a few weeks, we could find Mother and move on. Maybe I could even find a man I *liked* and *wanted* to get naked with to finish the job.

"Within hours, or so I've been told." He tilted his head and I suddenly felt as if I was being pandered to. Obviously, he'd never left a female unsatisfied. Permanently. "I will take very good care of you. You have my word."

Damn. I'd just have to hope I was a one-day kind of girl. But I suspected I was more likely the four-day variety. "Let's go, then."

I must not have looked overly excited about it—which was pretty much how I felt—because Faith put her hand out to stop me. "Wait."

"What?" I asked, wanting to get this over with so we could get on with finding Mother.

"You don't have to go with him. God, this is ridiculous. Why would you go off with a guy you don't like and have sex? It's just... weird. Wrong. There's five other guys. The second one's cute."

The guards glanced at each other, most likely trying to figure out which one of them was the 'second one.'

"She's right, Trin," Destiny added. "It's like getting your v-card punched. Don't just do it to get it over with."

I rolled my eyes, then leaned toward Faith. Destiny stepped closer so we were in a huddle. "Imagine using your vibrator and you're close, really,

really, close to coming. Riding the edge... and the batteries die."

Destiny made a funny whimper sound. We might all still live at home, but we were full-grown adults. We had vibrators and boyfriends and sex and real lives.

"That's what I feel like. All. The. Time."

Faith bit her lip and gave me a look of pity. "Then pick one. There are six guys. One of them's got to be appealing to your hysterical Va-Jay-Jay."

I couldn't help but laugh. I stroked my hand down Faith's long hair and we turned as a unit to stare at the men. All six of them. The consort was appealing, but not appealing enough. Destiny was right, the second guard was really hot.

The consort looked irritated now, as if we were not only insulting him, but were idiots as well. "With all due respect, ladies, the guards will not be able to service you as you need. Only a male who has met The One, whose cock has been awakened by his true mate, can be of service to a female. Even then, we consorts have lost our mates. My mate died two years ago in a tragic accident. I am the only one here whose body is awake and fully functional. None of the guards are mated. And Aleran males do not have sex with other females while their mates still live. I will not allow you to ask another male to dishonor his mate in this way. I am but a lowly consort, but my purpose is sacred and valued on all of Alera."

Great. We're here for all of two minutes and we already insulted every Aleran we'd met.

"My apologies, Cassander. We did not intend to insult you or the guards. I would never ask a warrior to dishonor his mate. Never." I glanced at the guards. So did Faith and Destiny. Those big, hot guys, who had to be similar in age to the three of us, hadn't had sex? Hadn't had their cock *awakened?* Mother had mentioned it, explained it, but I hadn't believed her. I mean, every guy on Earth from like fourteen on was as horny as hell. They thought only of sex, of getting into a girl's pants from the moment they woke up until going to sleep.

And these five guards had never felt lust? Or had sex? Never had an orgasm?

"Holy shit," Destiny whispered. "A planet of hot virgin males. Every woman's fantasy."

"It's the consort then, Trin," Faith whispered. "Just close your eyes and think of Justin Timberlake."

I laughed. Faith had always been obsessed with the pop star. Determined to make the best of an awkward situation for all of us, I walked toward

Cassander, who bowed and kissed my palm. It was warm. Pleasant. No great rush of lust fired me up at the simple touch, but I didn't need a great lust. Or true love. I just needed to get this alien Ardor taken care of—as quickly as possible—so we could go track down the kidnappers and save Mother.

Besides, we weren't going to get naked right here in the transport room, so at least I had a little time to have a chat with my vagina. She'd have to make peace with the plan. Because I didn't have time to search this planet for a mate. Every minute that passed was one more that Mother was in mortal danger.

Leo

I ARRIVED at the transport center with ten minutes to spare, but stopped short when I saw five guards with Lord Jax's insignia on their shoulders enter the center via a side door. Walking with them was a consort I recognized. Cassander of Jax was well-loved by the ladies. In fact, I had heard tell of males becoming frustrated when their new mates complained that Cassander was a better lover.

Of course, he'd had more than twenty years with his mate before she died. I could only imagine the skill and knowledge he held in regards to a female's body and her desires. He would know exactly how to touch her to make her surrender to his every demand, every need.

I had no doubt that should I ever find The One, I would make sure to satisfy every single one of her needs. Her cries of pleasure would become my obsession. I would play her body like a master, watch every move and every breath until I was her master, until she begged for my touch. Craved it. Couldn't come without it.

In my pants, my cock stirred as a strange scent teased my senses.

My cock stirred. All on its own. What the fuck?

All because of a delicate fragrance, like the translucent petals of the Aleran flower that grew in abundance in the citadel gardens I'd played in as a boy. Crazy.

It had been years since I'd been to the citadel and should not be stirred by simply inhaling the soft scent. Even longer since I'd been fool enough to bury my nose in the center of the silken petals and breathe in their scent. When the queen lived and ruled, I'd played in the gardens while my father went to meetings with the other guards. But the citadel, while in the same city, was far from here and I'd not passed by those sacred gardens on my journey from my guard post. Perhaps the wind brought the scent to me, cloaked in darkness, a taunting ghost of happier days.

Strange. I hadn't thought of those long, bright days for years. But the smell of the flowers lingered, as if clinging to my body with a mind of its own. And to stir my cock? A *scent,* not a female. Perhaps it was time to see a doctor.

"Stop daydreaming and get moving, soldier." I whispered the order to myself. There were three females inside that building and I'd promised Prime Nial to protect them with my life. I had no idea who they were, or why they'd traveled all the way from Earth. But those facts were irrelevant to me. I didn't need to know their names to die for them. That was a warrior's vow. To die for innocents he or she had never met. To protect them simply because they needed someone stronger, more skilled, to defend them from any threat.

Prepared to step out of the shadows and enter

the building, I stopped cold as three dark shadows caught my eye as they moved along the roof.

Assassins.

Within moments they'd vanished again, blending into the shadows as if they'd never existed. Phantoms. But I'd seen them. Knew they were real.

Knew they were hunting.

Fuck, there was no question as to why they were here. Why they were stealth and silent.

The Earth women.

Who *were* they? And where had the assassins come from? Surely not Lord Thordis Jax? From all I had heard, he was a decent and honorable male. But perhaps someone in his family was not. Or had assassins followed these females all the way from Earth? From Prillon Prime? Nial's mate, Lady Deston, had spoken as if the females were of great import to her personally. Perhaps whoever hunted these ladies wanted to get to Prime Nial, his second, and their mate. Then why were the females on Alera, not Prillon?

"Where did you go, evil bastards?" My voice was so quiet I barely heard the words as I scanned the rooftops and buildings for movement. I was not a trained assassin, but I was very, very good at killing. And watching. Waiting. I was hunting now.

The door opened as a vehicle pulled up to the side entrance. A large EMV slowed to a stop, and I watched as two guards exited the transport center, checked the vehicle and driver before leading the three females, the consort and the rest of the guards inside. The shuttle was large, but fast, moving past me in a blur as I threw my tracker into the air. The small, autonomous drone would fly just out of sight above them and allow me to follow their every stop and destination through the computer, displaying coordinates I could follow easily.

Racing to my own EMV, I quickly followed, frowned when I spotted a second drone tracking the shuttle. Lord Jax's vehicle was much faster than mine. Much more expensive. My soldier's wages didn't allow for such luxuries, nor did I care for them as long as the EMV took me where I needed to go. I was not frivolous. Depending on how far they traveled, I could remain right behind them, or be twenty minutes delayed.

The assassins, however, would surely have the very best EMV money could buy. They needed to monitor their prey, know exactly where they were headed. Follow. Attack. Kill.

Fuck. I tapped my comm and placed a call to

Thordis Jax. His bleary-eyed assistant answered the call.

"What is it? It's the middle of the night, sir. Who are you and why are you calling me?"

"I need to speak directly with Lord Thordis Jax. It's an emergency." I flicked a gaze from the drones to the rear of the Earth females' EMV.

"Hummph. No, it is not. Lord Jax is asleep, and I assure you, whatever your emergency, it can wait for a decent hour."

"Listen to me," I countered, tipping my tone low. "Wake him. Tell him his special guests have assassins following them."

"Who are you?" he asked instead of taking my command seriously.

"It doesn't matter. Wake him the fuck up and give him the message."

The older gentleman snorted again, rubbing his eyes, and I slammed my hand on the comm to end the call. Idiot. I didn't have time to argue, and I wasn't about to tell him who I was. Especially when I didn't know if this seemingly innocent old servant was, in fact, feeding information to Prime Nial's enemies. Prime Nial himself had said to trust no one.

I was on my own.

The assassins would beat me to their destination.

Already, the EMV carrying the Earth females was ten minutes out of range. I watched as they grew farther from me on my EMV's display. Fuck.

The assassins would not delay. They would complete their task, swiftly and without mercy, and disappear into the night. I could only hope I got there before all of the ladies' guards were dead.

4

Trinity, The Grande Penthouse, The Mytikas Summit Housing Complex

Besides being a gigolo, Cassander was also a tour guide. On our ride, he shared details about Mytikas, the large city we were in. It reminded me of New York or Hong Kong. Sprawling. Crowded. If it weren't for the fact the vehicle we were in was more *Buck Rogers* than Buick, it would seem like we were on Earth.

The same went for the hotel we'd entered. Swanky, like the Ritz. It even had a penthouse level. It seemed social status wasn't reserved just for Earth.

We were in a suite, with Vegas-worthy views. Lights and tall buildings were all that could be seen. I had no idea what time it was, but it was dark out. I didn't feel the least bit tired, although I was sure it had more to do with adrenaline than anything else. That and the constant, aching hunger I had to be touched. I felt like an addict who desperately needed a hit. Sex was practically all I could think about. My body actually *hurt.*

Maybe after a few orgasms, I'd feel better and conk right out.

"There are three bedrooms to your guest quarters, thanks to your host, Lord Jax," Cassander said, pointing to the doors off of the suite's central room. Decorated in soft colors, creams and tans, the suite was elegant and screamed wealth. Yeah, Lord Jax was definitely working it. Artwork graced the walls; abstracts I assumed were of Aleran landscapes, but it could have been the Grand Canyon for all I knew. If it weren't for the doors that swished open and closed automatically like in *Star Trek,* it felt familiar and... normal. As if Alera wasn't as culturally different from Earth as I'd assumed. "The guards will remain in the central room, assuring our safety while we are... occupied. There is a bedroom for each of you, my ladies. You and I, Trinity, will take this one."

Cassander was bold enough to take my hand in his and lead me in the direction he spoke. The touch was gentle, warm, but it didn't reassure me, only made me nervous. Yeah, a gigolo to ease my Aleran Ardor. Soooo different from Earth.

Faith came over to me from the window where she'd been taking in the view. "I'll pull one of these comfy chairs up here. Right by your door. If you need anything, I'll be... well, listening."

She blushed, and so did I. Like she wanted to listen to her sister having sex with a stranger. I winced, and apparently, Cassander saw my less than excited expression.

"You have nothing to fear with me. I promise you, my lady. You will feel only pleasure." His fingertips grazed the inside of my wrist in an act meant to be seductive. Instead, I felt annoyed. My body liked it, humming to life with sudden interest. But me? The battle going on inside my head? Angry, upset, *I hate this* me was definitely winning.

I glanced at Faith who bit her lip. I wasn't sure if she was trying to stifle a smile or keep from vomiting.

"Does that thing have real bullets or lasers or

what? And where can I get one?" Destiny asked. Faith and I turned to see our curious—and ruthless sister—tugging a space-age weapon from one of the guards' hip holsters.

"Um... be careful with that," the guard warned. He was the second guard, the hot one. Or, the hottest one, because none of them were bad-looking.

Destiny narrowed her eyes and tossed her purple hair back. She waved the gun around as if she were an idiot who'd never touched a weapon before. "What, you mean someone might get hurt?"

The guard blanched and reached for the weapon.

Destiny dropped the act and aimed the gun at the floor. "Easy, soldier. I was just playing with you." Her deft hands fiddled with it. "Stun mode. Fascinating."

Faith rolled her eyes. "She'll be entertained for hours." Faith's gaze traveled over the guards' uniforms, taking in the array of weapons, knives, blasters, and odd attachments that Destiny would, undoubtedly, dissect like a scientist. If there was a PhD in weapons, she'd have a plaque on her bedroom wall. Shiny and silver, I could just see it surrounded by the blast of purple bedding and purple paint on the walls.

"Yeah, giving the guards heart attacks," I countered.

"So forget about her. About us. What's going on out here. Just... do your thing." Faith pulled me away from Cassander, into a tight hug. Her lips were next to my ear, and her voice so low I was sure no one else could hear her. "I know you hate this. I'm sorry. But we need to find Mom, and we need you to survive long enough to help us do that. Okay. We're right here. We got your back. You know that. We got you."

Tears. Great. That was soooo not what I needed right now. "Thanks."

Faith nodded and stepped away, taking up her new position in the chair, guarding the hallway that led to the fuck-den. Sheesh. Was I really going to do this? Did I have a choice? Every moment since we'd arrived on the planet had made my Ardor worse. I didn't know if it was the alien men, the air, or what, but my Ardor had gone from the low simmer it had been on Earth to a full blown assault on my senses. I couldn't think. Could barely breathe. I wasn't a child. I could control myself, but I was miserable. Uncomfortable. Needy. My skin so sensitive that Faith's hug had made my skin burn with heat.

Damn.

I looked at Cassander and held out my hand

with all the enthusiasm of a criminal facing down a firing squad.

"We'll be right here, Trin. Right here." Faith assured me once more with a nod.

"Okay."

Cassander said nothing but took my hand with a gentle tug. I gave up, let him lead me into the bedroom. Oh, there was a big bed all right. Huge. White blankets and fluffy pillows all turned down, ready for entry. I felt like I was a virgin sacrifice as he closed the door behind us. Locked it.

"Wine, my lady?" he asked, going to a table and pouring a dark liquid into two glasses.

"Can't hurt," I said on a sigh, holding my hand out. I took a sip. Fruity wine burst on my tongue. It wasn't grapes that had been fermented, but something else. Still, it tasted good and I needed some liquid courage. And to loosen up.

I took another gulp as Cassander shrugged out of his jacket. Beneath, he wore a white shirt that was trim to his body. As if it was the most natural thing in the world, he unbuttoned the shirt and slid it down his shoulders and back. He was pure muscle. Step one in his seduction plan, wine. Step two, strip tease.

And I still didn't want him. Shit. I didn't feel all

too teased, so I had to hope he had toys in his arsenal, maybe in the bedside table, or a really wicked tongue. I took another gulp of wine, stared at the defined masses of muscle moving under his skin. He was built. Nice arms. Really nice backside. The way my pussy was pulsing and my breasts ached, I should have been all over him. I should just take off my clothes, lay down on the bed, close my eyes and let this man work some kind of magic on me.

He turned, his wine in hand and a sympathetic look on his face. Sympathy, and lust. So, I was what? I new notch on his belt? Oh, look at the famous consort who got to fuck the future queen? He didn't know that, but I did. And I was not feeling this.

I glanced at the bed again and tried to imagine him pounding into me as I held onto the headboard. Or... put my head under a pillow? Kept my eyes closed? Turned off the lights?

I set the wine glass down on the bedside table, shaking my head. No, this wasn't going to work. There was no way in hell I'd let this guy go down on me, no matter how skilled his tongue. It would take four days of foreplay to get my mind as ready as my body for sex. And even then, the idea of him grunting and sweating and pumping into me just made me want to gag. No. Casual sex wasn't my thing. Never had been. So, this stupid alien body was just going to have to shut up and deal for a while.

Yeah, my girl parts were eager for a big cock. But, they didn't rule me and they were going to have to be a little more discriminate than an alien prostitute. They'd just have to chill the fuck out.

"Look, Cassander, I'm sure you're really great at your job. Total stud and all, but I can't do this. I'll be sure to give you a great review, but sometimes a girl's just got to say no."

He looked appalled. Shocked. Like I'd hit him with a stun gun kind of amazed. Had no one turned him down before? God, his ego must be huge.

"But, my lady—"

His wrist chimed. Glancing at it, he stiffened impossibly further.

"What's the matter?" I asked, looking from his wary eyes to his wrist.

"There's, um... a threat. A warning has been sent."

I stilled, my heart leaping into my throat. He might want to bang me, but right now he was the guy who knew his way around Alera. He had a wrist thingie that sent him stuff like those fancy mini-computer watches on Earth. If he said there was a threat, I believed him. I was the visitor here and had to trust him, at least in this.

"Let's go in the other room with the guards." He held his arm out signaling me to precede him. "I need to give them this update." I walked toward the door, but didn't make it two steps before the room's window shattered. I scrunched my shoulders up and ducked down near the door, my hands instinctively going to my head. A dark figure swung in. Covered heat to toe in black, he hung from a wire *Mission Impossible* style.

Holy shit.

"Run, my la—" A blast hit Cassander in the chest and he crumpled mid-word as I scrambled to open the door. His second blast hit the door above my head and I crawled on all fours into the hallway as Cassander bellowed behind me. I heard a scuffle. Another shot. I slammed the door, screaming for my sisters.

"We're under attack! Run!"

That's when I saw Faith crouched down behind her chair, a dead guard on the ground next to her. Destiny was screaming obscenities around the corner, out of sight.

"Faith? What are you doing?"

Faith turned to me, her eyes round with fear. "You know I don't kill things."

I closed the distance as the sound of several shots were fired in the living room area. The explosion of glass made Faith cringe and she peeked around the corner. "Ouch. That was a nice table."

"Seriously?" I pulled her back, out of my way, and took a quick glance around the corner. One guard was still alive. One. But he was hurt. Bad. Blood was pooling under his head on the nice, thick cream-colored carpet, but he was still breathing. And my sister, Destiny, was bleeding, circling, looking for an opportunity to get in a killing blow to one of the bad guys. It wasn't the guy who came through the window after me, so that meant there was more than one. She leapt forward, locked in hand-to-hand combat, moving so fast I couldn't keep track of her motions.

Faith peeked up over the chair next to me. "Jesus, our sister is scary."

"Shut up and get in there." I hadn't forgotten about the attacker in the bedroom. And I had no idea if Cassander was dead or alive.

"What? No way."

"There's another one coming from the bedroom," I hissed. Pushing to get her moving, I scrambled around the dead guard on the floor and took his weapon as we positioned ourselves on the other side of the chair. “You keep track of Destiny. I’ll watch the hall.”

Inspecting the weapon in my hands, I frowned. I knew the basics about handguns—Destiny had made us at least go to the firing range with her a few times—but this wasn’t a weapon like anything I’d ever seen before. Shit.

The bedroom door opened and I pushed Faith. Hard.

“Trin!”

“Move!”

The mask had been ripped from my attacker’s head and I could see his face. His hair was dark, his eyes a brilliant green I’d never seen before. His forehead was bleeding from a deep cut—one point to Cassander—but I wished he was still covered up because now I could see his eyes, the grim turn of his curled lips, and all I saw on his face was death. If I saw his face, that meant he had no intention of keeping us alive to identify him. I’d seen enough crime scene shows on TV to know that.

I lifted the gun and pointed it at the assassin. His eyes narrowed, but he kept walking. I squeezed the trigger, or whatever it was. Nothing. Crap. How did this thing work?

"Shoot him!" That was Destiny. How the hell she knew I was facing down a killer, I had no idea. She was a freak with eyes in the back of her head.

"I can't get the gun to work!"

Destiny took a punch to the gut, distracted by my situation. She punched back, hard, swinging and connecting with her opponent's jaw. "Safety on top, not the side. Orange light."

I followed her swift instructions, or tried to, pressing on the orange glowing area. The light turned a pale, pale green. I lifted the gun again, but it was too late. He was on top of us, pulling a very big, very long knife free from the sheath strapped to his thigh. I screamed.

"Shoot him!" Faith yelled, kicking the nearest chair into him to buy us some time.

I fired. A blast of light, or laser, or whatever, shot from the gun. Direct hit in the chest. He just smiled.

I fired again. Again.

He looked amused now. Either there was some weird setting on the gun or he was wearing an alien version of Kevlar.

Shit.

The door exploded inward with a boom that

made my ears scream in pain. I squeezed my eyes shut, but knew the bad guy was right in front of me. I couldn't avoid him. Faith dropped to her knees, covering her head.

The assassin looked away from me, toward the door, and all amusement faded from his eyes. I might not be a threat to him, but whomever destroyed the suite's entry door sure was.

5

Leo

"SHOOT HIM!" A woman shouted on the other side of the door, followed by the sound of repeated blaster fire.

I didn't wait, setting a charge on the locked door for three seconds. Moving to the side, I closed my eyes, weapon drawn, and counted.

Three. Two. One. Long fucking seconds.

The explosion rocked the hallway, the lights above me flickering off then back on as I burst into the room.

I took it all in with a sweeping glance.

A female—with strangely colored hair—was fighting one of the assassins.

A second assassin was dead on the ground, surrounded by four dead guards. The difference between good and bad was easy to distinguish; the guards wore identical, and familiar, uniforms, the assassins all black. Their faces were covered.

Another guard, the lone surviving one it seemed, was crumpled on the ground, trying to reach for his blaster, the blood under his head meant he'd most likely black out before he got it.

The other two females were on the far side of the room from him, crouched behind a chair, one firing a weapon on a third assassin.

He whipped his head around toward me at the sound of the blast and my entry, clearly confident the female's blaster shots would do him no arm. Our eyes locked.

I knew that face. I narrowed my eyes at him, and he all but dared me to attack. Bastard. Prime Nial had been right to call me. I doubted either of us expected danger to come upon the females so swiftly after their arrival, nor from this band of evil. It hadn't been more than an hour since their transport. These females held some kind of power, something very powerful people were willing to kill to contain.

"Get down!" I yelled at the females, hoping they would listen. Raising my own weapon. He wore protective armor, but that would not stop me from killing him with a precise shot to his head. I frowned when the assassin turned and ran, disappearing down the hallway where I assumed there was a bedroom.

I had no doubt the consort would be found there, dead. Had the female's Ardor been slaked first? I doubted it based on the timeline of events. There hadn't even been time to disrobe, let alone fuck an Ardor away.

The two females near the chair ignored my order the moment their attacker was gone and stood, turning to the third female, still locked in combat.

Fuck. Two were seemingly safe, but the third was in trouble.

"Kick him away from you!" I yelled as I dashed toward her. The assassin was much bigger than she and I was surprised she'd held him off so long.

She heard me, delivering a hard, swift kick to the assassin's abdomen and stepped back, out of range. Purposely giving me the shot. I lifted my weapon, aimed.

"Don't kill him!" A female near the chair screamed the order, but I ignored her command. This particular band of assassins was too dangerous to remain alive. He had to die. One of them had already escaped. I wouldn't lose two.

He was armored, as I knew he would be. I fired at his chest anyway, momentarily halting his movement. That was all I needed to take the head shot.

He dropped like a rock. Remained still. The female he'd been fighting stepped forward, bent arms raised, hands fisted tightly as if she were ready to keep fighting, and kicked him in the side with heavy black boots, just to make sure I'd gotten the job done.

"He's dead. I assure you," I said, coming up to stand beside her.

She turned to me, glanced up, her purple hair flying. Her eyes were a bright blue, and completely without fear. Her pupils were dilated, but it seemed more from the rush of fighting than fear. She was small. Her odd clothes couldn't hide the curves of her gender. And she'd just fought off one of our planet's deadliest assassins.

It seemed Earth females were brave. Bold. Fierce.

But why were they here? Now? And why did someone want them dead?

"Who are you, and what do you want?" The voice washed over me like the burning heat of a fire and my cock stirred. Again. Just as I'd felt earlier. No, not just stirred, but thickened. Lengthened.

Shocked, I turned swiftly back to the females near the chair. One had long brown hair and large, dark eyes. She looked warm. Soft. Too gentle to be the female who'd spoken in such a commanding tone.

My gaze shifted to the other.

Holy. Fuck.

Instantly, I bowed low to the most magnificent female I'd ever seen, but I kept my eyes on her. I couldn't look away if I wanted. Golden hair surrounded her head and shoulders in a silken wave I couldn't wait to touch. Her eyes were a deep, intense blue, and staring me down, analyzing my every move. Her lips were a soft pink I longed to taste, to feel wrapped around my cock.

My fingers twitched at my side and I cleared my throat to disguise the groan of need I felt building like an explosion within my body as my cock came fully erect. Pressed against my uniform pants, which had suddenly become ridiculously too small. I was rock hard, long and thick, but now? Gods, now it was as if I had a pipe growing larger and larger down the inside of my thigh. I'd had no idea how erect I would get.

For the first time in my life, I ached. I wanted, no *needed,* to get closer to her. To get her naked and needy and screaming my name.

Just one sentence from her and I knew. She was mine. The magnificent creature staring me down over the top of a blaster was *The One*. My mate.

Fuck.

My earlier thoughts of remaining a bachelor soldier were all but forgotten. I inwardly laughed at my ignorant self. I would never be alone again because I'd never let this female out of my sight. Or away from my touch.

The clothing she wore did nothing to hide her form. Trim pants that were blue, worn and faded as if she didn't have an S-Gen unit available and wore this pair again and again. A shirt that bared her arms. While tall and lean, she had ample curves. Round and soft in all the right places. I could nuzzle and lick, grip and even spank.

And she'd almost been killed by fucking assassins. I saw red, wished I could kill the one all over again, race after the one who'd escaped.

My protective instincts roared like a caged monster, the remnants of the attack, the bodies on the floor, the blood, the *threat to my mate* taking on colors and intensity I'd not felt moments ago.

Mine.

Trembling with equal parts rage and need, I dropped to one knee and bowed to the female I would devote myself to for the rest of my life. "I am Captain Leoron Turaya. Prime Nial asked me to protect you and assist you in any way I can. I am sorry I arrived so late to the battle. Are you well?"

"Prime Nial sent you? What's the code word?" my mate asked, one pale eyebrow raised. She didn't lower her weapon. I didn't blame her, for she was smart to be cautious. She should trust no one. No one but me, but she hadn't learned that yet.

I lifted my head, gazed up at her. Confused. Code word? I searched my mind and found what she sought. Prime Nial's mate, Jessica, had said something strange about Trinity's favorite food being code. Now, I understood. "Strawberry ice cream."

I had absolutely no idea what I'd just said, some strange Earth term, but all three females relaxed. My mate put the weapon down and I noticed her hands trembled. That would not do. She shouldn't feel anything but happiness. Peace. I longed to take her into my arms and offer comfort, but she wasn't safe here. None of them were. The assassin had fled, but he'd be back for her. His kind didn't leave a job unfinished. If these three were as valuable dead as I assumed, the next attack would be more cunning. And brutal.

Over my fucking dead body. I was at war with myself. The need to protect and defend battled with the need to stand, walk to The One and pick her up, keep on going until she was pressed against the nearest wall. My mouth on hers, my fingers working open her strange pants, seeking her center, finding it hot and wet for me. Sinking into her. Finally.

My cock didn't understand danger, my body demanded action even knowing my mate could be harmed. My need would not lessen, and neither would the size of my hard cock, until I'd spent in her. Made her scream my name. Not once, not twice, but many, *many* times.

The warrior in me pushed through, wrested control from the primal, rutting instincts fighting to rule me. For now. "You are not safe here."

"No shit." The purple-haired female kicked the corpse at her feet again before reaching down and divesting him of his gear. She was efficient, systematically checking every pocket and pack, everywhere the assassin had hidden anything of use to him. She looked up from her work at the other two.

"Help the guard while I get weapons and intel. Get busy." She waved the weapon she held as if dismissing them to do she commanded.

The dark-haired female moved to the injured guard and pulled a small blanket and pillow from one of the chairs. I thought she would cover him, but instead took a knife from his gear and cut the blanket into bandages. Dropping to her knees, she tied them around his head wound to stem the flow of blood. She deftly wrapped his wounds completely and placed his head on the pillow before looking up at me. "Do you have 9-1-1? You know, paramedics or someone who can take care of him? Someone to call? A doctor? Hello?"

While I heard her words, I didn't immediately process she was talking to me. I was too stuck on The One, the curve of her cheek, the color of her lips, the upturn of her nose. I shook myself out of my cock-induced trance and nodded, pulling a ReGen wand from my belt, pushed the button so the blue, healing light glowed. It was too small to correct all of the damage to the wounded man, but it would stop the bleeding until he could get to a ReGen Pod. It was better than nothing—and all I had. "Yes, we do. But wave this over his head for a minute, and it will keep him alive until they arrive."

She frowned and stared at the device as if she'd never seen one before, then began to move it a few inches over the guard's injured head as I'd instructed.

"We should leave quickly. The assassin who escaped will not run and hide. He is a killer. It is not safe for you here."

"Obviously," the dark-haired one grumbled. "We need a place to hide until daylight."

"I know. I will take you somewhere safe. But no more public places. I don't want anyone else to know you're on Alera."

"Amen to that." The purple-haired woman moved on to her third body, stuffing weapons into a blanket she'd tied into a carry pouch. She stripped Lord Jax's guards and assassins alike, missing nothing. One-track-mind, that one.

I came to my full height, eager to be closer to my mate. I took one step before our gazes locked. Held. It was as if there weren't bodies littered on the floor. No hint of danger, or a deadly assassin who might return to finish what he started.

For the briefest of moments, it was just me. Her. *Us.*

My cock pulsed, heavy. My balls tightened and I felt a spurt of pre-cum seep from the tip. Yes, I was truly awakened. My cock wanted this female and it wanted her now.

I had to get her away from here. Away from any danger, then I could allow the eager brute to do the thinking for me.

She tilted her head to the side and licked her lips, looking me over as if her desire was as strong as mine. Bright color flagged her cheeks, her eyes wide, searching. Roving. Perhaps I would be blessed with a lusty mate, one as eager to claim me as I was her. I didn't care who she was or what planet she was from. She was mine.

"Who are you?" she asked, her voice losing the commanding tone, replaced now with something akin to wonder.

I knew just how she felt.

"Leo," the purple-haired female replied before I could. "He knows the code word. We should go. You guys can... whatever, later."

That female began to annoy me with her impatience. Didn't she know I'd been waiting my entire life for this moment? For my cock to stir for The One? That my life had changed irrevocably?

I didn't look away from my mate, yet I knew the logic was sound.

"I am Leo, captain in the royal guard, servant of Alcra. I fought with Prime Nial in the Hive wars. I am here to serve you."

Serve you in so many ways. Gods, I wanted to kiss her, lick her and know the flavor of her skin, breathe in her scent, taste her pussy, make her come and then sink into her. Mark her as mine. So I would be completely and truly *hers.*

I thought of the assassin still at large. Of the continued threat to her. This was no longer just a life debt owed to Prime Nial. This was my mate. The One. She was in danger, and I would stop the fucking rotation of the planet to keep her safe.

The brown-haired female smiled up at me from where she continued to treat the guard, with blood covering her delicate hands. She, too, wore odd, worn clothing. All three of them were. They had on pants in blue or black, simple shirts, my mate with strangely short sleeves. Who kept their arms bare this high in the mountain regions? Was it extremely hot on Earth? Was it a style to bare her body for others to see?

The purple-haired one had on sturdy dark boots, the calm one shoes with straps that barely covered her feet. My mate wore white cloth shoes with laces. Simple, worn, a bit dirty and smudged along the edges, as if she weren't one for extravagance. I didn't need expensive garments or jewels to decorate my mate. I wanted her bare, every perfect inch of her pale skin visible, only to me. To see the life flow through the pale veins beneath the skin, to run my fingers along them.

"So, Prime Nial saved your life?" the quiet one asked. "And now you're saving ours?"

I nodded. I would die for my mate. Kill for her. Stop at nothing to protect her, claim her. But they didn't need to know that. Not yet. "Something like that. We must leave." I held out my hand to my mate, hoping and praying to the goddess that she'd touch me. She did not.

She did look at me, though, and my cock wept some more at having those beautiful eyes on me. "I'm Trinity." She angled her head toward the dark-haired one with the funny, strappy shoes. "This is my sister, Faith. And that's her ass-kicking twin over there, Destiny. We just need a safe place to stay tonight. Okay?"

"And some food," Destiny added. "Kicking ass made me hungry."

I glanced her way, said, "Are you sure you don't need more weapons?"

The comment was meant to be sarcastic, but Destiny looked up from the unconscious guard she was separating from all of his battle implements. I noted that she was careful not to jostle his head or the pillow Faith had placed so carefully beneath him.

"Seriously?" she asked, looking up at me. "Hell, yeah. What do you have?"

"He's kidding, Destiny," Trinity told her. A beautiful name for my beautiful mate. She shook her head and rolled her eyes. "If the guard is stable, let's go."

Destiny scrambled around to the guard's other side, but my mate was not amused. And apparently, she was in charge, even though the purple-haired one was so bossy. Fascinating.

"Now, Destiny," Trinity added, her tone going quite commanding. Fuck, that was hot. "Come on, Faith.

"Let's go before more ninja assassins show up," Trinity added as Faith stood and handed me my ReGen wand.

What was a ninja? Was that a special band of assassins on Earth? Had they faced such danger before? The thought made me shudder with relief that they were here, with me, under my protection. I didn't think the assassin would show his face again tonight, but I would not lower my guard until we were somewhere safe, somewhere only I knew. And I would employ every tactic I'd ever learned to make sure the threat couldn't follow us tonight.

"Fine," Destiny countered. "I got enough stuff for all of us." She stood and held out a blaster.

"I don't want it," Faith said, holding her blood-stained hands up in front of her.

"Tough." Destiny shoved the blaster into Faith's chest and held it until her sister slowly, reluctantly wrapped her fingers around it.

"I hate you sometimes," Faith said.

"Only when you know I'm right." Destiny slung the blanket full of gear over her shoulder, raised a questioning brow at Trinity—who held up the blaster she'd been using when I took out the entry door—and stepped up beside me. "Let's go, Leonardo."

"It's Leoron."

My mate sighed and tucked her weapon into the pocket of her strange pants. They, along with her shirt, fit snugly to her lean frame. They did nothing to hide her figure, the curves I would soon have my hands on. "Let's go. I can't take much more."

We carefully climbed through the twisted metal of the destroyed entry door. I had no idea if there were other guests on this floor, but I had to assume they'd fled after the explosion.

In the hallway, Faith gasped, turning to my mate. "What about Cassander? Did you, you know?"

The consort. Fuck. While it was his job, I couldn't think about that rich bastard touching Trinity's skin. Kissing her. Licking her sweet pussy. Filling her—

"No." She sighed. "But, he's... dead."

I nearly shuddered with relief. Not at his being dead, but at him not touching my mate. I clenched my fists at my sides. Perhaps it was good he was no longer alive, for I'd have killed him myself if he'd laid a finger on her. Consort or not. It was completely irrational. I hadn't known of Trinity's existence hours ago. Now, the thought of another male touching her made my blood boil. But, it also meant that Trinity was the one with Aleran Ardor. Who needed to have her pussy filled, to be soothed with orgasm after orgasm.

Goddess, she would not need a consort. Her

mate was here, available and had an eager cock. She would not go unsatisfied. Ever.

"Oh, shit. Now what are we going to do about your little problem?" Destiny asked.

"It's fine." Trinity waved a hand through the air as if it were nothing. Either she was minimizing her condition or 'it's fine' meant something different on Earth. Ardor was not a joke, taken seriously by everyone on Alera. Clearly, these females didn't know what Trinity would be in for if she didn't get it under control.

"I wasn't going to sleep with him anyway. It was too weird." She scrunched up her nose as if something smelled bad. "I told him—"

"What? Told him what?" Faith asked. All three of us waited for Trinity's answer, but me most of all. Did she have a male back on Earth? Was she already mated to someone I could not seek out and kill with my bare hands?

Was she hurting? Needed my cock filling her? My mouth on her skin?

I was shaking now, struggling to breathe as the sweet scent of her drifted to me once more. Aleran flowers. Sweet. Ripe. Mine.

She looked years too old to be suffering from the Ardor. Most females on Alera were well past that stage around their twentieth year. My mate looked at least five years older than that. A woman. Mature. Sexy. Stunning.

Trinity shook her head. "It doesn't matter. I'm fine. I'll be fine," she insisted again in a tone of voice that implied she didn't want to be argued with, although I could see because of her tight blue pants that she rubbed her thighs together. No, she ached, her pussy throbbing with the Ardor heat, but was being brave. My sweet mate. "Anyway, he's dead."

"We're screwed," Destiny added, frowning.

"In more ways than one," Faith said, glaring at me. "I *told you not to kill him.* We needed him alive so we could interrogate him and know why we're being targeted."

I blinked. What? These three were interrogation experts?

"The assassin? Absolutely not. He was going to murder you," I bit out. I had no intention of telling them that I knew the assassin who had escaped. Knew the price he demanded could be paid by very few. Until I knew who these three were, I wasn't going to share. I needed something to exchange with them. Information they wanted for what I wanted. I glanced at Trinity. "All of you."

Destiny actually snorted. "As if. I totally had that guy."

"And the one in the hallway?" I pointed in that direction. "The one who escaped? Did you have him as well? Or would he have killed your sisters while you played soldier?" I'd saved Destiny's life, eliminated the threat to her, as any honorable male would do, and she was chastising me as if I were a child? No.

"Touché."

She grinned up at me as Trinity watched the byplay with a completely unreadable expression. Was she overcome by her Ardor? Overwhelmed by what had just happened? Afraid?

I would reassure her, set her mind at ease. Make her worry for nothing, not even her orgasms. I couldn't wait to make her melt. Burn. Scream my name.

I had no idea what Destiny's response meant, this word, touché, nor did I care. She was cooperating. That was all I needed at the moment.

"Come with me," I told them, finally getting all of us away from danger. My cock was a terrible leader. I had to get my head back in control, at least for the moment. I didn't know what threats were outside this floor, this building. Even down the street. "Keep your heads down. Don't look up. There are vid stations everywhere." I led them farther down the hall. Thankfully, Trinity stepped into place directly behind me, close, where I needed her to be. Destiny brought up the rear, her weapon at the ready, and I was surprised to realize I was reassured with her in that position. She was a warrior and my mate trusted her. A strange female, but a capable fighter. I would take all the help I could get. Anything to get my mate far from here. Safe.

And naked. Very, very naked.

6

Trinity – somewhere in Mytikas City

"Do you have any idea where we are?" Faith asked, looking around.

"As if we know where we are on Alera when we're *not* in danger?" Destiny countered in her usual snarky way. Destiny leaned back, inspecting the windows and frame, knocking on the material in some bizarre ritual I didn't even want to guess at. "I like your ride, Leo. I saw the windows are tinted. Is this bulletproof glass?"

Leo had taken us in his own vehicle, after walking a random route for several blocks to ensure we weren't followed. It wasn't as fancy or large as the one Lord Jax had provided, but I hadn't cared if it were a horse and buggy. As long as we were moving further and further away from danger, at least for the time being, I'd felt better. And having him sitting beside me in a closed area—even with my sisters as chaperones—had been intense.

Leo's hands moved with confidence over the controls. "We do not have metal projectiles in our weapons. But the windows are military grade. Nothing can get through them, not even blaster fire." He looked over at me, his gaze lingering, making me squirm in my seat.

Was he as hot for me as he seemed? Or was I reading something into his expression that wasn't real. Was my Ardor warping my mind?

"This is a standard military issue EMV. Nearly indestructible. No one can see inside. You're safe. I assure you."

"How fast does this thing go?" Faith asked.

"This *thing* obeys all driving laws so that we do not attract unwanted attention." He was so serious. His face set like stone. His jaw tight. Everything about him screamed powerful, alpha male. Warrior.

I'd wanted to crawl over and into his lap, straddle his thick thighs and feel the huge cock that was in his pants rubbing against me. To kiss him, taste him. I'd had to bite my lip to stifle a whimper as I breathed in his scent—a temptation that had filled the vehicle. Dark, rugged. I wondered what the sheets of his bed would smell like. Would that scent wrap around me and make it hard to breathe? Would I drown in him?

Did I want to?

Yes. Right now, god yes. I did. He had to have pheromones pumping off him in waves, for I was so close to coming that I ached. God, I was desperate to rub my clit, to get off, but I knew it wouldn't help.

I needed him. His touch. His mouth. His hands. His energy. His alien cock and all that sweet alien cum. Maybe if I humped him, rubbed our bodies together with our pants the only things between us, that would be enough. Would my body be satisfied with that?

Hell no. That was the answer. I wanted naked. Grunting. Thrusting. I wanted him to shove me up against the wall and take me as hard and fast as he could. I wanted to ask him to do it. Beg him. *Beg.*

Then I realized I was going insane, envisioning dry humping a guy—an alien—that I'd just met as he drove across a huge city... with my sisters watching. I wasn't sure what disturbed me more, that

I wanted to go at it with a complete stranger, or that I didn't care if my sisters watched.

Jeez. This Ardor was serious business. Mother had said it could lead to insanity, even death, if left unsated. I'd laughed at her. Now I realized my mistake. My body wasn't my own. Not right now. And I didn't like that lack of control one little bit.

So I tried to forget my eagerness to fuck Leo and thought of our attackers. It was obvious we'd hit a nerve with someone on Alera, that Mother's kidnapping had definitely been carried out by an Aleran. We weren't supposed to be here. We would cause massive amounts of trouble for whomever had taken her. While I was glad to know our existence would piss someone off, I wasn't really thrilled about being shot at.

From the back seat, Faith leaned forward, squeezing my shoulder. "Look, Trin. Look."

Her slender finger pointed out the window to the brilliant sparkling light that our mother had described to us, but we'd never seen. Shimmering like holographic glitter, the queen's light shot into the dark sky like a beacon. It was bright, brighter than the full moon on a cloudless night, and I had no doubt it could be seen for miles and miles. Maybe even from space.

And the light still burned. Mother was alive. For now.

"She's alive." Destiny whispered from the back seat.

"Of course the queen is alive. Somewhere. But it's been almost thirty years since she's been seen. Most think she was captured and is sitting in a containment cell somewhere, rotting. Most have lost hope that she will ever return." Leo, all but forgotten in the driver's seat, supplied the information. I tore my gaze from the citadel, and that all-important light, to watch the emotion, or lack of, cross his face.

"And you? What do you believe?"

"I don't waste time thinking about these things. I follow orders. I'm a soldier. That is all."

"Bullshit." I couldn't take it, not with my pheromones going crazy. The complete lack of expression on his face was going to make me throw things.

"The queen disappeared when I was very young," he offered. "I remember her, remember her laughter, her beautiful gowns, the way she would tussle my hair when my father attended meetings with the king. But that was a long, long time ago. Decades. If she were alive, she would have returned by now. Saved us all from years of war."

"Years of war? What war?" I didn't want to know. Not really. Mother had tried to talk me into returning years ago. Before law school. But I'd been selfish. Didn't want the responsibility that came with being a queen. And too scared to leave the only life I'd ever known. Perhaps hadn't truly believed Alera really existed.

Oh, I believed now.

Leo's hands gripped the controls, his knuckles white, his hands and muscled forearms crisscrossed with dozens of scars. I wondered if the rest of his body was like that. "What war, Leo?"

He turned to me, allowed the car to shift into some sort of automatic pilot. "I'll tell you anything you want to know. But know this. You're mine. So if you get scared or want to run, want to leave, you can't. I'll fight to the death to keep you safe and happy."

"Leo." God, gorgeous Leo. I didn't know what to say to that. He'd met me a few minutes ago, and already vowed to keep me? Possessive, much? I knew —well, I'd seen—the evidence of his interest come to life in his pants. That huge, meaty cock that I wanted to ride so badly. But I didn't know who or what he was. Was he a consort, like Cassander? Had his mate died or was he really a virgin?

That seemed impossible. No woman in her right mind would be able to keep her hands off him. He looked like Henry Cavill's version of Superman, without the tights. The Aleran uniform he wore did nothing to hide his *Fittest Man in the World* physique. He had to be six-four, with broad shoulders and a narrow waist. With the weapon holster on his hip, he gave off that aura of chivalry, as if he were a space-age version of a knight. He wasn't in shining armor, but when he'd come through the smoking ruins of the suite's entry, I'd been mesmerized.

And my Ardor? It had gone insane. Hot all over, my pussy had literally flooded with arousal. My mind went all *gimme, gimme, gimme.*

Now that we were away from danger—at least temporarily—I didn't have to split my attentions. Faith and Destiny could try and figure out who the assassins were, but they weren't going to get far. Not on their own. Or, at least, not tonight in a strange city.

The vehicle entered a private parking facility and Leo told us all to duck down so the camera attached to the security gate wouldn't record our presence when the window slid down automatically.

After the scanner flashed over his eyes, a

computer voice thanked him and the window went back up, and he drove into the lot.

"It's safe now. They don't allow cameras in soldiers' quarters."

"Why not?" Seemed to me, it would be the opposite.

"Code-breakers once infiltrated the vid system and staged a perfectly executed attack. Took out an entire city division of royal guards in one night. Over a hundred guards. Some of the oldest. The best. The code-breakers knew where everyone would be. Where they slept. Where they ate. What time they came out of their rooms. After that, no more vids."

Hackers. On another planet. Things weren't that different after all. How horrible. "How long ago was that?" I asked.

"About five years."

We rode a very plain, dark gray elevator and ran into no one. We hadn't gone to a penthouse this time, only five floors up. Instead of a hotel suite, Leo had taken us to a small apartment. I looked around. Living room, a library, two bedrooms, a kitchen—although it had appliances I'd never seen before. It wasn't fancy, more... comfortable. Was this Leo's home?

My sisters were looking around. Faith staring out

at the spire, clearly visible from the largest set of windows, and Destiny scoping out exits and entry points.

Everything was normal.

Except me, and this relentless lust making my brain mush and my body about as useful as a lit match thrown on a bonfire. I looked my sisters over, took in the dried blood that clung to them still, acutely aware of the warm, strong male hovering just a few steps behind me, locking the door. "Are you both sure you're all right?"

Faith nodded and looked at Destiny. "We're fine, but how about you?"

"I wasn't hurt."

Destiny rolled her eyes. "We know you weren't injured, but what about your other problem?"

I squirmed, my desire thrumming. My nipples were hard and sensitive, my padded bra only adding to the irritation. I wanted to rip it off, all of my clothes, my skin irritated by the fabric, by being confined. I wanted to climb Leo like a monkey, but I wasn't going to *admit* that. We were close, too close. They did *not* need that kind of ammunition.

Destiny leaned in, whispered, "I mean, it hasn't been cured or fixed or whatever."

It was as if she were worried Leo could hear us.

He was walking around the apartment now, doing a security sweep, even though it appeared safe to me. He wouldn't have brought us here otherwise.

I trusted him. I had no idea why I should trust him over the five guards who'd been sent to protect us, but I did. Obviously, someone on Alera had been tipped off about our arrival. We'd either been followed from the transport center or one of Lord Jax's people was a traitor. Perhaps someone at the Brides Center on Earth? Warden Egara? That idea was crazy, but I was quickly learning we shouldn't trust anyone.

Except Leo. He was safe. I knew it down to my bones. He was the one, the only one who I felt could protect us from whatever evil had taken Mother, and wanted us dead.

But I had no right to ask him to risk his life for me. For us. For a woman who'd run, abandoned Alera almost thirty years ago. He'd said he didn't waste time thinking about it, that he resented my mother for leaving her people, for causing so much death. So much war.

How could I sleep with him, use him, and walk away? I had a job to do. A duty to the people of Alera and to my mother, and that did not involve risking the life of a humble soldier. He was a good one.

Honorable. Simple. How could I tell him who I was when he hated my family? My mother? His past. He'd suffered. For years. And it was partially my fault. I could have returned more than five years ago. I could have spared him some of those scars.

"Shit. I don't know what to do." I whispered the words, my hands up to cover my face from a sister who would say far too much.

When I didn't answer her question directly, Destiny continued, "Look, I know we all want to go find Mom and fast, but we need to chill out for a while. I mean, we transported all the way to Alera. Today. We were attacked. Today." She held up her bloody hands. "I'd say we need a little downtime."

Faith nodded. "I need a shower. A bed. *You* need Leo."

Destiny grinned and waggled her eyebrows. "And he needs you. Did you, um, see his cock? It was literally tenting his pants."

Faith giggled. "One look at you and... bam." Faith held up her hand and raised her pointer finger in a 'just a minute' sign. Or, an example of how a guy's cock went from down to up. Very, *very* up.

I hadn't missed it. Not at all. Especially since all that... maleness seemed to be because of me.

Not Faith or Destiny. While he'd interacted with

both of them, he'd barely given either much more than a second glance. As for me, he practically devoured me with his eyes.

And back to his cock. God, it was, well... huge. His uniform pants had done nothing to hide the thick, long bulge. Had I said thick and long? Even the outline of the wide crown had been obvious. He'd been aroused. Instantly and thoroughly aroused.

"Cassander said a guy didn't get hard unless he was with a woman who was The One. That the five guards had yet to find their mates, therefore their cocks were... impotent?"

Faith laughed. "That's a weird word. Leo doesn't look impotent at all. Maybe dormant. And Trinity, my dear, it seems you've got what it takes to *awaken* Leo."

I was attractive. I didn't flatter myself to think I was gorgeous, but the fact that I'd supposedly awakened Leo sexually was pretty empowering.

"You know what, guys?" I replied. "My Ardor isn't better and I *really* want all that untapped desire focused on me. He's gorgeous and—"

"A virgin," Destiny added.

God, a virgin hottie who wanted me. Blatantly. I whimpered because I was soooo ready.

"You are safe here," Leo said, coming back in the room. We spun about as a unit, and I felt guilty talking about him. He was more than a virgin. He was a Coalition fighter who'd saved our lives. Brought us to safety. He was honorable and wise. Chivalrous and brave.

All that and a big cock, too.

His eyes immediately met mine, but I couldn't hold his dark gaze. Nope. It dropped to the front of his pants. Yup, a hard-on of epic proportions. I had no idea how he was able to walk comfortably.

I pointed. I couldn't help it. "Um... should, does it, I mean—"

Instead of being embarrassed—like an Earth guy would have been for being caught so blatantly aroused—he stood straighter, rolled his shoulders back, which only made his cock more pronounced. "It's for you."

I'd never seen a man so... intent. His dark hair was mussed from battle, his uniform stained and torn by the shoulder. He looked rugged and fierce. My palms itched to run over him, feel the hard muscles, well-defined beneath his clothing. And to feel that cock, learn every ridge, every bulge. Every long, thick inch.

Seeing it made me feel feminine and powerful.

Even in my jeans and sneakers, my hair most likely snarled and wild. Oh, and an inside-out shirt. Yeah, totally sexy.

I heard Faith stifle a laugh, but didn't look away.

"Buster, on Earth a guy doesn't show that much interest until at least the end of the first date." Destiny's words had that punch of abrasiveness I was used to.

"On Alera, a male's cock will only rise for The One." He was so earnest about it. If an Earth guy had said that, it would have been the worst line ever to get in a woman's pants.

But here, he meant it. *All* Aleran males were this way. Just like I had my Ardor, he had his… stirring. But I could fuck anyone, even Cassander, the gigolo. It seemed I really did have the power to *awaken* Leo.

God, that was hot.

"See?" Destiny muttered, in response to his statement. We'd been right. "Are you telling me that you've never had a hard-on before?" Destiny asked, blunt as ever. Thank god she was thinking the same thing. I couldn't dare ask.

"No."

"You've never…" Faith asked, twirling her finger around in circles.

His fists clenched at his sides, his breathing

coming deeper, his chest rising and falling as a result. His eyes blazed, focused right on me, his jaw clenched. I could relate. I was practically coming out of my skin holding myself back. Any thought about not jumping his bones was gone. I wanted Leo and I wanted him now. Holding me, pinning me to the wall, pressing me down.

"No."

How hot was that? He'd been waiting for this moment, for me, to come all the way across the universe. To *awaken* him.

"But now?"

"I wish to be alone with my mate. To soothe her Ardor."

Leo took a step toward me, but no further. That was it. I couldn't wait any longer. I needed him. Needed his hands on me. His mouth. His cock.

Now.

I launched myself at him, my arms going about his neck, my mouth meeting his. He opened for me, his tongue finding mine.

His hands went to my bottom squeezed. I jumped and wrapped my legs around his waist.

"Okay, then," I vaguely heard Faith say. "We'll just... um, be... elsewhere."

I didn't notice anything else after that besides

Leo. His taste, his scent, the hard feel of him. Everywhere. My pussy was pressed against the hard length of his cock and I rocked my hips into him. His tongue was in my mouth, licking, learning. My hands were tangled in his silky hair, holding him right where I wanted.

He tore his lips from mine. Growled. God, he looked so fierce, possessed even.

"Mine," he uttered, his voice deep and rough, and carried me down the hall to a bedroom, kicking the door shut behind him with enough force that the pictures on the wall rattled.

Oh yeah, I was totally his. For the first time since my Ardor kicked in, my pussy and I were in complete agreement.

7

Trinity

My back bumped into the wall and now I was pressed between two very hard things. One cold, one hot. Scorching hot. His hands moved from my butt and over me, my thighs, my waist, my breasts.

"I can't wait, mate," he murmured as his hands molded, weighed and played with my breasts through my t-shirt.

I moaned and arched my back. His hands felt so good. Big. Hot. Gentle, considering how wild this was.

"This first time will be hard and fast."

Ya' think?

Through barely opened eyes, I could see how much control he was using. I needed, but god, Leo *needed.*

I had a momentary thought of the Atlan guard at the Brides center. Was this what his beast was like? Wild and... beasty? No wonder no one ever heard of a divorced Atlan woman.

"Hurry." One word was all it took. He lowered my feet to the floor and made quick work of my pants, opening and tugging them down my legs. His hands went to the front of his pants as I stepped to try to get my feet out of my crumpled jeans, but only had success getting them off one foot before Leo lifted me up again, this time his big hands on my bare ass. They were so big they cupped me from hip to crease.

I hooked my legs around him once again, felt his cock, hot and hard, nestled along my pussy. Bare and pulsing. Thank god for the birth control injection Warden Egara had given me at the bride center, because I didn't think I could stop. And I didn't want to. I wanted him hot and naked, skin on skin. I *needed* his seed inside me. I needed his energy, his wildness to fill me up.

"Are you wet for me? I will not take you unless you are ready."

I rocked my hips, coated the length of him in my arousal. "So wet," I murmured. Everywhere our skin touched was like a mini inferno. My flesh heated beneath his hands. My body was hungry for him.

His eyes met mine. Fierce desire. Possessiveness. Intense control. Need. I saw it all in that one instant. I wanted this. I wanted him. Deep. Hard. Thrusting so hard my back never left the wall.

Without looking away, I felt his hips pull back, his cock shift so it was notched right at my entrance.

God, I could feel how big he was, the crown parting my lower lips. I held my breath, waiting. Waiting.

With one word, "Mine," he thrust up into me.

I groaned. He growled.

The hand on my butt squeezed, and I knew I'd have little bruises there in the morning. His other hand slapped against the wall by my head as his eyes fell closed. A red flush crept up his square jaw, his lips thinned, the cords of his neck went taut.

But lower. God. His cock filled me. Stretched me. Opened me up like no other. I could feel every hard inch of him. So impossibly deep I sucked in my breath. Squirmed.

My pussy clamped down on him, squeezed, milked, tried to pull him deeper, which was impossible. My clit pulsed as it rubbed against him. My heels pressed into his ass as I held him to me. And inside, something shifted, something hungry and desperate and primitive roared to life inside me and screamed for more.

"Mine." That was my voice, but one I didn't recognize, as I wrapped my arms and legs around him in a viselike grip. Energy, raw, male, covered me like warm, melted caramel, the heat going straight to my clit. To my pussy.

My core clamped down. Hard. Squeezed his cock like a fist.

He groaned. Pulled out. Thrust deeper. Harder. He held me there, riding his cock, stuffed full. Unable to move. Not wanting to. "Fuck me, mate. Take it. Take it all." He ripped open my shirt and his, pressed our bare skin together. Pressed his lips to my neck, my cheek, tasting my flesh, devouring me like he'd never get enough. And every moment, heat filled me up. Energy. Hot. Erotic. Like a drug I'd never get enough of. Every cell was hungry for him. My entire body a living flame.

This was why I'd come to Alera. *This* was what a human man could never give me. What I needed.

He pulled back. Thrust so hard my breasts bounced. I tilted my head back, giving him better access, unable to resist. Not wanting to. I had no choice now. My body wasn't my own. It was his.

"Oh my god," I gasped. It had never been like this. *Never.* And he wasn't even moving. I was so close to coming I couldn't catch my breath.

His head was buried in the crook of my neck and his hot breath fanned my skin. My fingers ran through his sweaty hair. My nipples were hard, aching for his hands. His mouth. Anything he could give me. And my body was already taking him in, demanding his life force, his strength, and I knew that I would never be the same.

For the first time in my life I felt... alien. *More* than human.

This was raw and dirty. The basest form of fucking, and he'd only thrust into me a few times. It was as if he'd been dreaming of being inside a pussy. Just that and nothing more. He held himself frozen, as if *this* connection alone was so pleasurable he didn't need more.

Well, I did. I'd been desperate to come for weeks. Ached. I'd been on the brink, close to the edge but with no way to jump off. But now I had it. Now I felt whole, as if Leo's hold was all that was keeping me together, that once I gave over to the feelings, they'd be so intense I needed him to hold me together, ensure I didn't break into a thousand tiny pieces.

With the slightest shift of his hips, I came.

My head went back and I screamed, clawed, clenched. Milked.

I had no doubt Faith and Destiny heard, and probably everyone else in the building.

He pulled back once, then thrust deep and followed me over. A jagged sound, like a beast coming unleashed, ripped from his throat. His entire body went taut and I could have sworn I felt his cock thicken even more before he spent. Filled me with his seed. The warmth of it coated my insides as even more raw heat poured into my flesh, filling me with so much power, so much energy that I came again, the pleasure pushing me over for long minutes. When it was done, the aftershocks continued to rock me as muscles in my core pulsed randomly, out of sync, caressing his cock—almost as if my body itself was thanking him.

"I could die happy, Trinity. Right now. Inside you."

I smiled and held him closer, running my

shaking fingers through his hair as my pussy continued to pulse and twitch around his length. Happy that he didn't appear any worse for wear for the energy I'd felt pouring from him. That he'd found pleasure as well. And that for the first time in months, I wasn't about to crawl out of my skin with need.

That was his first orgasm, the first sexual pleasure he'd ever felt. And he'd found it with me. *Inside* me. Because of me. I wondered if we were truly more than just Ardor and a male's awakening, if this intense chemistry would lead us to something more.

If I was ruined for all other men.

Yeah, I totally was.

I had no idea how long we remained locked together, unmoving. Savoring. It had been so incredible, I didn't want him to pull away. Or out of me. Our skin was sweaty, our breaths ragged. Eventually, our muscles relaxed, our grips loosened, but Leo still kept me pinned to the wall. As if we were anchored together and if separated, we might fall.

He lifted his head, looked at me. For the first time, I saw that his dark eyes were no longer plagued. There was a contentment, a softness to them.

"Hi," I whispered.

The corner of his mouth tipped up. "Hello, mate. That was… incredible."

"So good," I agreed.

"If you think that was good, just wait until I have you in a bed. Naked. With hours to test all the forms I learned in training."

"Training?"

His grin made my entire body break out in goose bumps. "Oh, yes, mate. Every male on Alera has weeks of classes on how to pleasure our mate. Centuries of learning handed down from generation to generation. And I cannot wait to test every single one of them on you."

Oh yeah, that sounded like a good idea. My pussy was soooo ready for round two. "Okay."

He smiled fully then and… wow. It was the first time I'd seen him smile, seen the full impact of *him.*

I was devastated by his looks. Eyes that didn't blaze with fury, but with heat and simple satisfaction. A nose that had a slight crook and had been broken and hadn't been healed by one of those wand thingies. A square jaw with dark whiskers. I envisioned him with a beard, but a better thought popped into my head. Him between my thighs, that scruff against my tender skin as he used his wicked, wicked tongue...

"That can be arranged."

Without any effort, he turned and carried me to the bed, lowered me to it.

He stood before me, tall and proud, and I took him in, legs parted, hand gripping the base of his cock. He'd only opened his pants enough to get his cock free to fuck and now the material was bunched around his hips. But his cock... it was huge. And still rock hard. He'd just come not three minutes earlier and he was still ready.

Did I say huge? Like porn star big. No wonder I'd whimpered when he thrust up into me. My inner walls, now empty, clenched with eagerness for more.

But, he'd been a virgin and no doubt had plenty of pent-up need to still be so hard. With his grip about the base, there were inches... *inches* of the shaft above it. Glistening with my arousal, proof I'd been as eager for him as I'd said. It was a ruddy plum color, thick veins bulging along the length, as if it had a vital, never-ending supply of blood to keep it hard. The tip was flared, broad and fluid seeped from the tip as if he'd never stopped coming.

His balls hung large and heavy, a blatant sign of his virility, of all the seed he had to give me. Of the amount of it that slipped from my pussy even now.

"You're in bed, mate. Time to get naked," he said, his tone laced with command.

He expected me to strip for him as he watched, stroked himself.

Totally worked for me. While I'd come—and come hard—my Ardor had been soothed slightly, but not completely. Otherwise, I'd be unconscious right now after an orgasm of that magnitude.

In our haste to fuck, I'd somehow tangled my jeans around my left sneaker, so I reached down and worked it all off, let them fall to the floor. Coming up onto my knees on the bed, I tugged the remains of my t-shirt off, reached back and removed my bra, tossed it over his shoulder.

I'd never seen such an appreciative gaze from a man before. He looked at me reverently, yet full of sexual heat. Completely lacking in modesty, as if he wanted me to watch him. Needed my attention. His fist stroked him harder, faster and his hips bucked once.

He came with a caveman grunt, a thick spurt of his cum arced and landed on my thighs.

"Goddess save me," he said as he knelt there and

rubbed his seed into my skin. It wasn't sticky like a human man's, more like massage oil. The indescribable scent filled my head and I leaned back, arching into his gentle touch, wanting more. Wanting it all over me.

"More, Leo. I need you again." I reached for him, wrapped my hand around his *still hard* cock, grateful he didn't appear to need time to recover. I didn't want to wait.

When he caught his breath and let his hand fall to his side, his cock was *still* hard, still aiming straight for me.

"Obviously, I have little control with you," he said. "You're too lovely. Seeing your breasts, your pussy, my cum coating it. You are very beautiful, mate. Perfect."

I licked my lips, wondering how he'd taste—not only his cock but his chest, the tips of his fingers... every inch of his skin—and I swayed toward him, licking my lips. It was as if he were a drug and I needed another fix.

"No. It is you who needs tending," he said. "To come until your Ardor is soothed."

I did feel better after the orgasm, but not completely sated. I wanted more. I was eager for it. Primed, even. But Leo, in all his newfound prowess, had been a virgin until a few minutes ago. I got a sense of his bossiness, but his cock would be ruling him now. He'd be like a teenage boy.

I was the experienced one here. If I wanted him to do something, I'd have to tell him. Or... I could show him what I liked, for how else would he know. I had no doubt he'd like it, too.

"Get naked and get on the bed," I said, practically repeating his words.

He eyed me for a moment, thinking. Perhaps a female hadn't bossed him around before? Tough. My pussy had needs and I was going to take them—and him—into my own hands.

He stripped at record speed and I settled on the bed, watching as he showed me everything. Muscled shoulders that made me sigh. Tapered waist. Thighs thick as tree trunks. And that cock, pointing straight up at the ceiling.

"How long do you think it will take for you not to spontaneously come when you see me?" I asked, smiling at him. I was teasing, but also serious. We couldn't leave this apartment if he would come in his pants if his cock was out of control.

"If I don't breathe in your flowery scent, see the way your nipples tighten beneath my fingers or the way your pussy opens to my cock, then tomorrow."

"And otherwise..."

His hands gripped the blanket, his eyes roving over me as if he couldn't get enough. "Otherwise, perhaps the day after. Or next week, all depending on how many times I take you. Make you scream with pleasure. Watch your eyes glaze over as you come, as you milk my seed. Make me yours. Take my joining energy. I will come inside you mate, over and over, until you can't hold any more. Until you don't need. While you can have any male of your choosing, as your mate, I will take you until can't think of anything but me."

My pussy clenched at the idea of him coming again and again. And again.

"Well, let's see whose need is sated first," I replied, crawling over to him.

His eyes flared at the position, at the way the tip of his cock nestled against my lips. I licked the flared crown and he groaned, burying his fingers in my hair. Urging me on.

"What are you doing, mate?"

I grinned. "I learned a few things, too."

Lifting up, I hovered over his cock, then lowered my open mouth down, one delicious inch of him filling me at a time.

The bedding ripped in his hold when I swallowed, sucked. Teased.

With one strong tug on my hair he lifted me and I rose up on my knees, finding his mouth with mine for a kiss that went on and on until my pussy was weeping, aching. Throbbing.

"Leo."

"I know what you need." Before I knew what was happening, I was on my hands and knees and he thrust into me from behind.

The new position—his huge cock—filled me even more. Stretched me as he wrapped his hands around my hips and lifted me off the bed so he could kneel behind me. He positioned me, my legs splayed outside of his.

"Put your hands around my neck and don't move them without permission." His order was almost a growl but I complied without thinking. His cock felt so good. His skin pressed to my back. My thighs. So much skin. So much heat. His body was feeding mine once more. Lighting me up on the inside. Making me burn. Want.

I'd do anything he wanted, as long as he didn't stop.

"Leo. God. Please." I lifted my hands back up behind my head and locked them around his neck, tugging on his hair in a silent demand that he hurry. Move. Thrust. *Fuck me.*

He moved one hand to my breast, holding me in place as he pumped up into me, lifting his body and mine. The other hand? I rocked my hips, whimpered as his fingertips found my exposed clit and rubbed. Played. Rolled the small nub between his fingers.

"This was lesson nine, mate. Do you like it?"

"Nine?" Lesson? What was he talking about? I couldn't think. I wiggled my hips, tried to lift and lower myself, anything to make the building tension ease.

His very male, very satisfied chuckle barely registered as he toyed with my nipple and sent his hot breath into my ear. "It was always the most intriguing to me. So much freedom for my hands."

He fucked me. Slowly. His cock moving like a slow-burn engine until the rhythm became the center of my universe. My existence. There was nothing but him. And his hands. His mouth on my shoulder. My neck. His heat and energy filling me up, just like his seed would.

"Come, mate. Take me in. Make me yours."

His order was a whisper, but my body heard him, felt the hard demand of his fingers on my clit. My body arced as if struck by lightning and he held me close as I shattered, lost my mind. Became nothing more than sensation.

He held me together, and I took everything.

His seed was a hot jet inside me, his growl music to my ears. He was mine. Right now, he was mine, and I wasn't finished with him yet.

8

Leo

"I STILL DON'T UNDERSTAND why someone left you something at the citadel," I grumbled, driving down the deserted roads. There were few vehicles this late at night. Everyone was in bed, where I should have been. With Trinity. "It's just an empty relic now. Multiple royals have entered and found nothing. And you won't even be able to get inside."

"Don't worry about it, just get us there alive. Okay? That's all we need." Trinity's voice was crisp, clear. Confident. Strong.

I loved hearing the power in her, knowing I'd helped make her that way.

Naked. Inside her hungry body. Filling her up.

In the two days since her arrival and my awakening, I'd fucked her until my cock was sore and my body completely drained. Every male on Alera knew the stories about the females' Ardor. The need for both seed and energy our females were born with. Now, I was part of her. Would remain part of her forever. Our life force mingled. My energy nourishing her cells, preparing her to be a mother, to have children, to be strong enough to survive.

When I was a younger man, I'd believed the honor of easing a female's Ardor was a violation. The idea of giving part of myself, part of my body, my very life force to a female had sounded like a burden.

How very wrong I'd been. Buried in Trinity, her hot, wet pussy milking my cock, the sweet scent of her skin, the soft silken strands of her hair—the sounds she made as I pleasured her.

Not enough. I'd give her everything. Kill for her. Die for her. Give her every last drop of my blood, my seed and my soul. My cock ached, but remained hard and hungry. I knew her now, knew from the way she squirmed in the seat next to me that she was far from satisfied. She needed more. Wanted more.

From me. Only me.

She'd said we fucked like rabbits, but I had no idea what that meant. I hadn't given her much time to talk—about anything—before I'd had my mouth on hers, quieting her except for her moans of pleasure.

And now I was a tiny bit sorry I hadn't given us more time to talk because I was taking the females to the citadel. To collect *something* that had been left there for them. Why the citadel? Did someone leave a package behind a shrub? That seemed unlikely, for the guards who circled the revered building had little to do but watch for strange people, strange packages. Anything out of the ordinary. In the past twenty-seven years, *nothing* had been out of the ordinary.

The spire still glowed brightly. The queen was alive, but silent.

Would this *thing* they needed to collect still be there? I'd definitely delayed Trinity long enough for their item to be found and confiscated. The three of them seemed confident that it was there. They were adamant, refused to go anywhere else.

"I still don't understand why you're here, on

Alera," I added, circling back to the first question I'd had about them since Prime Nial contacted me.

"You complaining?" Trinity asked. She placed her small hand on my thigh, and I had to fight the instinct to pull the vehicle over and fuck her right here in the car. Now.

I glanced at her, saw the curve of her lip and I knew she was in a teasing mood. If her sisters weren't sitting behind us... I'd tug her ankles so she slid down on the seat and I settled over her. It wasn't a big vehicle, I was only a Coalition fighter after all, but the cramped quarters would only be to my advantage as I fucked her. I could push off the side and take her hard and deep. And with her leg over the controls, she'd be wide open. Wet.

"Easy, soldier," she whispered.

"You guys have had two days to work this Ardor and awakening shit out of your systems," Destiny grumbled from the back seat. "Chill."

"You're the one who told me to jump him," Trinity countered, squeezing my thigh.

Jump? She had all but flung herself at me. I couldn't help but grin. "The strongest females on Alera have been known to awaken to Ardors that last up to a week. And Trinity is not yet appeased." But fuck, the last two days had been amazing, touching her for the first time. Tasting her lips, feeling the heat of her pussy against my cock, even through our clothing. The tight peaks of her breasts against my chest. "Thank you, Destiny, sister of my mate, for advising her to, as you say, jump on me."

"You're welcome. But I didn't do it for your blue balls. I did it for Trinity's vagina."

Trinity glanced over her shoulder at me. Grinned. "My vagina thanks you, too."

"What are blue balls?" I asked.

They laughed. All three of them. The NPU wasn't needed since we all spoke Aleran, but every once in a while, they added an Earth term that did not process. In that moment, I realized something and set the vehicle to auto.

"You're speaking Aleran. All three of you."

Trinity frowned and I could see the V in her brow with only the lights from the passing buildings lighting her face.

"Yes," she replied.

"But you're from Earth." The NPU wasn't processing and translating directly to my brain. We were all speaking the same language.

"Yes," Trinity added.

Up to this point, Faith had remained silent.

"Wow, Trin, you're a killer in bed if it took him this long to start asking questions."

"We know she's a killer in bed because we heard it all," Destiny added. "It's not like they were quiet."

I should have felt embarrassed. Possessive even, for Trinity's sounds of pleasure belonged to me. Instead, I felt pride that I could make my mate feel so much satisfaction. As expected, Trinity was not a virgin and had shown me what she liked. I'd been all too eager to combine what the male classes had taught me on pleasuring a female, but knowing my mate liked my mouth on her pussy, that flicking the left side of her clit made her come within seconds. That there was this little spot deep in her pussy, when I pressed firmly as I sucked on her clit made her scream, made her so wet she dripped over onto my palm. That she liked it from behind the most out of all the positions we'd fucked. So far.

No, I wasn't embarrassed. I was aroused. My cock was uncomfortable and thick in my pants and ready for more. Ready for Trinity. I was completely at her mercy.

And that was why I was driving them to the citadel in the middle of the night instead of driving into Trinity's pussy. She'd asked if I would bring her —all three of them—to the citadel. It had taken a day for me to agree, and even then I'd agreed on the condition that we visit in the dead of night. I promised to protect them, keep them safe and they wanted to go to the most exposed—and revered—place on the planet.

Only when I was deep inside her did I agree. Oh, she'd used her female wiles to manipulate me. What male could deny his mate anything when she had her fingers pressed to the smooth spot behind my balls? She'd teased me with light touches until I agreed, and then she'd gotten me off.

It was only after my head cleared that I added the requirement that it be done late at night.

"I may be completely at your mercy, mate. I may have these *blue balls* you mention. I may even need to pull over and fuck you once again because I can't control myself. But I am not stupid. I am well aware you are redirecting, keeping me focused on the scent of your pussy, the feel of my cock inside your body, the wet heat of you milking me of cum, instead of answering my questions."

"Holy shit, Trin. He's a dirty talker," Faith commented. "I like it."

Trinity's hand gripped my thigh now. Hard. Yeah, she liked it when I was crude, when I told her exactly what I wanted to do to her.

"Yes," Trinity replied, her eyes on mine. I wasn't sure if she was saying yes because she wanted me to get between her thighs and breathe her in, to get my cock nice and deep so she could all but draw the cum from my balls, or if she was admitting she was intentionally avoiding a response.

"I have been accommodating, mate. To you and your sisters." I spoke the truth. They had been safe and protected. Bathed and fed. They each wore Aleran clothing generated in my quarters, using my S-Gen machine. I had done everything they asked of me...and they'd told me nothing.

"Not us, hot stuff. Just Trinity," Faith added, but I could tell from her tone and the smile on her lips she was playing.

I wasn't. While I couldn't force my cock to go down, especially not with Trinity beside me, I *could* focus on something besides fucking. "We are almost to the citadel. I've done as you've requested. My assignment with Prime Nial is to offer protection and assistance in whatever you need to do. But in order to fulfill that, I must be briefed. Now."

The queen's light could be seen glowing above the buildings. We were only a few blocks away.

"Leo—"

I took Trinity's hand from my thigh, moved it

away. "Don't Leo me. I will give my life to keep you safe, but I must know everything."

Trinity eyed me, bit her lip. She glanced at her sisters. "We have something to get at the citadel."

"Yes, you've said that. What is this *something*?"

Trinity turned in her seat to face me, one knee bent. "I don't know. None of us do. That's the truth."

"Then why is it so important, so dangerous, that someone wants you dead?" I thought of the assassins the other night and my grip practically strangled the controls. We'd avoided danger, so far. But taking the three females out into the city, exposing them to the world, made me edgy.

"I don't know."

I clenched my teeth to keep from snapping at my mate, demanding she answer me.

"We don't, Leo," Faith added.

"How do you know where it is? It's not like there are places to hide something around the building. It is all open, with guards."

"Our mother told us where to find it."

"Your mother. On Earth." This was hard to believe.

"Yes," Trinity added.

The road we were on went directly to the citadel. The silver building could be seen in the distance before us, the glowing spire a beacon. We were a hundred feet from the guards, not close enough to raise an alarm, but being such a late hour and without anything to do, their attention was on our vehicle.

My frustration grew and I ran my hand through my hair. I wanted to wake up Prime Nial, force him to tell me more. It would be easier than prying the answer from these three stubborn females. Surely, they could handle the most ruthless of interrogators.

"Mate," I growled, and not in a sexy way. "Where?" I couldn't ask more. It sounded ridiculous. *Where did your Earth mother tell you a secret package was hidden at the heavily guarded and fortified citadel on far-off Alera?*

"Inside."

A bark of laughter erupted and I stopped the vehicle in the middle of the street. There was nowhere else to go.

"Is your mother trying to get you killed?"

Trinity frowned, crossed her arms over her chest. She no longer wore the Earth garments, but an Aleran outfit I'd created using the S-Gen machine in my quarters. She didn't look like she'd come from Earth any longer. She'd blend in perfectly on Alera, which was exactly what I wanted. To blend in so the assassins wouldn't have such an easy target.

"Of course not."

"Are you sure she doesn't want you dead? Because there's no way you can get into the citadel with the protection the ancients left behind. They created an energy field surrounding the inner sanctum. No one but their descendants, those of royal blood, can pass without being destroyed. Instant death, mate. I've seen it happen twice, right after the queen disappeared. Two of her less-blooded, greedy cousins tried to get inside. They wanted the throne, the power for themselves."

"What happened?" Faith asked.

"Cellular disintegration. A heat so hot it's cold. An explosion so fierce it doesn't need oxygen. The body explodes, but implodes. Dust." It had been years since anyone not of royal blood had tried to enter the citadel, and even then, it had only been those who wished to end their life, not ascend to the throne. "The clerics guard it night and day to stop others from attempting to end their own lives."

"Jesus, the citadel is a suicide mecca?" Destiny flopped backward in the back seat and put the weapon she'd been cleaning on her lap. "Didn't see that one coming. That really sucks."

Trinity didn't blanch, didn't even flinch at what would happen to her if she attempted to cross the energy field. "We must go to the citadel, Leo."

"Tell me why?"

"I can't. I made a vow to my mother, to my sisters. I can't tell you, but I'll be back. I promise. I'll find you."

Find me? "What are you talking about?" I stared into sad eyes, eyes filled with regret and cold dread filled me even before I felt the hard end of a blaster pressed to the back of my neck.

"You're getting out here, Leo," Destiny said.

I stilled, looked to Trinity.

"We're going in. That's our mission. That's why we're here." She held my stare for a moment, and I knew true terror. She was serious. Dead serious.

"Are you insane?" I asked, my heartbeat quickening. "You can't go in there. You'll die!"

She shook her head. "We won't. Trust me."

"You will, though," Faith said. "You're a nice guy. We like you in one piece. Especially Trinity. And I think she likes one *piece* in particular."

"Faith," Trinity groaned.

I noticed a few of the guards were slowly walking toward us. Their weapons were aimed at the ground and their stances indicated they were not at fight readiness. They didn't fear someone could get inside the citadel, the protective energy field left by the ancients took care of that. Their role was part ceremonial, but also to keep the peace, if required.

At this time of night, our vehicle was an oddity and they were most likely bored. Still, they were walking this way and I had an ion blaster aimed at my head.

"Get out of the car, Leo," Trinity said. "Please." She tagged on the last, practically begging. The last time she'd said that word was when I'd teased her with my cock, settling the tip just inside her wet entrance and not going any further.

"I won't leave you," I countered. "You're my mate. I won't let you do this. And as a fighter, as I've vowed to Prime Nial to protect you. I refuse."

I heard the click of the weapon's fire safety being released, the high buzz of sound as the weapon held its charge, ready to fire.

"You'll have to kill me, Destiny."

I felt the sizzle, the heat of the blast as it went through my body.

"Or stun you," she countered.

I went stiff, every muscle in my body going rigid, then relaxing. I couldn't move anything.

"I'm so sorry," Trinity murmured, stroking my

hair, my cheek.

"Trin, open his door!" Destiny said quickly, but calmly. "The guards are getting closer."

Even frozen, I could move my eyes, watch as Trinity glanced out the front window. Reaching across me, she pressed the button to open my door. It slid up quietly. The guards stopped, thirty feet away.

Trinity didn't move all the way back to her seat, but stopped, her face right in front of mine. I could see every freckle, every worry, fear, doubt. "I'm doing this to save your life. I'm sorry. I really am, but we have to go. My mother's been kidnapped, and I really don't have time to explain or argue. We have to get inside." She leaned over and placed a warm kiss to my lips. "I'll find you when I can. I'm so sorry."

I tried to speak, but only a strangled groan came out. I tried with all my might to lift my arms, to grab her, to keep from doing this. But nothing worked.

"Trinity!" Destiny shouted.

Trinity pushed me out the door.

I fell to the street on my side, a whoosh of air escaping my lungs.

I was bent at the waist and I could see Destiny's big boot, then the rest of her leg come over the back of the seat. She dropped into the spot I'd vacated.

She looked down at me, her purple hair wild. Trinity was leaning forward, looking at me, her teeth pressed hard into her lower lip.

"You want answers, Leo. You'll get answers. Right now," Destiny's promise was more a challenge, but all I could do was watch as Faith waved good-bye from the back seat, Trinity took out her weapon, and Destiny lowered the door, once more hiding them from view.

I fought to speak. To yell. To tackle my mate to the ground and spank some sense into her. My brain worked and worked, but the stun still had a hold on me.

I could do nothing but lay on the street and watch as my vehicle picked up speed and drove right at the approaching guards. Destiny didn't stop and the fighters jumped out of the way, then fired at the back of my vehicle. The other guards, now realizing there was an incident, were running and settling into their positions, bracing for some kind of attack.

The stun wore off, from one heartbeat to the next, and I was up on my feet and running toward my mate. "Trinity!" I bellowed as the vehicle approached the citadel. Then closer. They were driving straight at the energy field.

I stopped. The guards stopped. Watched. Waited.

No one had ever driven a vehicle through the barrier before. Would it be disintegrated along with the occupants?

My heart stopped, I held my breath, watched as Destiny drove straight through, as if she had a death wish—or knew, she wouldn't die.

The vehicle skidded and swerved to a stop directly before the main entrance to the citadel. Tall doors, two stories tall.

Slowly, I walked toward the citadel, the guards beside me. Stunned, as I was, they'd all but forgotten I might be a danger. We watched as the doors to my vehicle—the vehicle that had just... fuck, just driven straight through the ancients' energy barrier—opened and three very *alive* females stepped out.

Destiny and Faith used their clothing to conceal their features and their hair. Only the curve of their hips and breasts gave away their gender. My mate? She did not hide. She stood proudly, her hair down, her stance wide. Hands on her hips. She stared up at the central tower, at the line of royal spires pointing to the stars in a magnificent display at its the peak. At the single spire that had burned bright since Queen Celene's time.

Trinity turned and faced me. Only twenty feet separated us now, but she might as well have been on another planet, because I couldn't get to her. The distance was small, yet impossible to breach.

Our eyes met. Held.

"Holy fuck, Trinity."

"You wanted answers," she called. She held up her hands, shrugged. "Now you know."

Destiny and Faith went around the vehicle and to the entrance.

There was only one possibility.

The guards were talking now, whether to commanders off-site or to each other, I had no idea. Nothing like this had happened in twenty-seven years and now it was my mate who'd crossed the barrier and lived. Who stood steps away from the citadel sanctum. From confirming once and for all who and what she was.

Royal.

The daughter of Queen Celene.

Destiny stood before the tall doors—there was no lock—and they swung open automatically, as if recognizing the one who requested entry and welcoming her. Destiny walked forward, disappearing into the dark interior of the sanctum. We all stood, staring. Waiting, knowing what might come next, what would prove them truly worthy. The blood on the sacred stone. The final judgment.

The second spire lit and everyone around me gasped. My heart skipped a beat. The added illumination was almost blinding.

Faith, who must have been holding off for the ultimate proof of Destiny's identity, followed. Just like her sister's had, Faith's face and head remained covered until she slipped inside.

After a minute, another light soared into the sky. Another spire came to life.

Another sign that would cause chaos and celebration. Perhaps ignite the spark of unrest among the noble families into a full-fledged war.

All this time, Trinity stood still, looking at me. Waiting. For what? My reaction? Forgiveness? Why hadn't she trusted me with the truth?

"This mother you spoke of," I called, the facts crystallizing in my mind now. No wonder Prime Nial wanted these females protected. "The one who told you there was something for you to retrieve at the citadel?"

She lifted her chin, took on a regal bearing that was genetically hers. "Queen Celene." She bowed to the guards, who looked as shocked, and numb as I was feeling. This simply was not possible. "My name is Trinity Herakles, daughter of Queen Celene and King Mykel, Princess of Alera."

I watched as my mate, a princess, walked into the citadel. I knew in a few moments my mate would place her blood on the sacred stone, that the citadel would judge Trinity worthy. When another spire shone bright into the night sky, her light all but blinded me, just as she had from the moment I met her.

I was nothing, just a simple Coalition fighter, a guard. I was not worthy of such a female, and yet, my body had awakened for a princess. The eldest daughter of Queen Celene.

My mate was heir to the throne of Alera. She would rule the planet.

If she survived.

And her comment in the EMV? About her mother being kidnapped?

Fuck. She'd been talking about Queen Celene. Her mother. Kidnapped by whom? When? Who would dare? And where would they keep her?

As if a spell had broken with her disappearance, the guards descended, stunned me once again. They weren't as considerate as Destiny had been, using a much stronger setting. Pain sizzled through every nerve and fiber of my being, but it was nothing to the pain of losing my mate.

I would find her. I would protect her.

Princess or not, she was mine. And maybe a hard-hearted ex-Coalition fighter was just the kind of monster she needed to keep her safe. Whether she wanted me to or not.

The world went dark. The four illuminated spires—one for the queen and one for each of her daughters—would alert the entire planet to their existence.

No more hiding. No more secrets.

Those lights, the beacons of hope, were the last things I saw as I lost consciousness and fell to the street.

Ready for more? Read Ascension Saga, book 2 next!

Leoron of Alera has learned the truth about his new mate's identity, but landed in the hands of her enemies.

The time for secrets is over…

Click here to get Ascension Saga, book 2 now!

THE ASCENSION SAGA

Thank you for joining me on this exciting journey in the Interstellar Brides® universe. The adventure continues...

TRINITY

Book 1

Book 2

Book 3

Volume 1 (Books 1-3)

FAITH

Book 4

Book 5

Book 6

Volume 2 (Books 4-6)

DESTINY

Book 7

Book 8

Book 9

Volume 3 (Books 7-9)

www.AscensionSaga.com

FIND YOUR INTERSTELLAR MATCH!

YOUR mate is out there. Take the test today and discover your perfect match. Are you ready for a sexy alien mate (or two)?

VOLUNTEER NOW!

interstellarbridesprogram.com

DO YOU LOVE AUDIOBOOKS?

Grace Goodwin's books are now available as audiobooks...everywhere.

LET'S TALK SPOILER ROOM!

Interested in joining my **Sci-Fi Squad**? Meet new like-minded sci-fi romance fanatics and chat with Grace! Get excerpts, cover reveals and sneak peeks before anyone else. Be part of a private Facebook group that shares pictures and fun news! Join here:

https://www.facebook.com/groups/scifisquad/

***

Want to talk about Grace Goodwin books with others? Join the **SPOILER ROOM** and spoil away! Your GG BFFs are waiting! (And so is Grace)

Join here:

https://www.facebook.com/groups/ggspoilerroom/

GET A FREE BOOK!

JOIN MY MAILING LIST TO BE THE FIRST TO KNOW OF NEW RELEASES, FREE BOOKS, SPECIAL PRICES AND OTHER AUTHOR GIVEAWAYS.

http://freescifiromance.com

ALSO BY GRACE GOODWIN

Interstellar Brides® Program

Assigned a Mate

Mated to the Warriors

Claimed by Her Mates

Taken by Her Mates

Mated to the Beast

Mastered by Her Mates

Tamed by the Beast

Mated to the Vikens

Her Mate's Secret Baby

Mating Fever

Her Viken Mates

Fighting For Their Mate

Her Rogue Mates

Claimed By The Vikens

The Commanders' Mate

Matched and Mated

Hunted

Viken Command

The Rebel and the Rogue

Interstellar Brides® Program: The Colony

Surrender to the Cyborgs

Mated to the Cyborgs

Cyborg Seduction

Her Cyborg Beast

Cyborg Fever

Rogue Cyborg

Cyborg's Secret Baby

Her Cyborg Warriors

Interstellar Brides® Program: The Virgins

The Alien's Mate

His Virgin Mate

Claiming His Virgin

His Virgin Bride

His Virgin Princess

Interstellar Brides® Program: Ascension Saga

Ascension Saga, book 1

Ascension Saga, book 2

Ascension Saga, book 3

Trinity: Ascension Saga - Volume 1

Ascension Saga, book 4

Ascension Saga, book 5

Ascension Saga, book 6

Faith: Ascension Saga - Volume 2

Ascension Saga, book 7

Ascension Saga, book 8

Ascension Saga, book 9

Destiny: Ascension Saga - Volume 3

Other Books

Their Conquered Bride

Wild Wolf Claiming: A Howl's Romance

ABOUT GRACE

Grace Goodwin is a USA Today and international bestselling author of Sci-Fi and Paranormal romance with more than one million books sold. Grace's titles are available worldwide in multiple languages in ebook, print and audio formats. Two best friends, one left-brained, the other right-brained, make up the award-winning writing duo that is Grace Goodwin.

They are both mothers, escape room enthusiasts, avid readers and intrepid defenders of their preferred beverages. (There may or may not be an ongoing tea vs. coffee war occurring during their daily communications.) Grace loves to hear from readers!

All of Grace's books can be read as sexy, stand-alone adventures. But be careful, she likes her heroes hot and her love scenes hotter. You have been warned...

www.gracegoodwin.com

gracegoodwinauthor@gmail.com